OPERATOR 5:
HOSTS OF THE FLAMING DEATH

SECRET SERVICE OPERATOR 5 ™
AMERICA'S UNDERCOVER ACE

HOSTS OF THE
FLAMING DEATH

By Curtis Steele

STEEGER BOOKS • 2020

PUBLISHING HISTORY

"Hosts of the Flaming Death" originally appeared in the August, 1935 (Vol. 5, No. 1) issue of *Operator #5* magazine. Copyright © 2020 by Argosy Communications, Inc. All rights reserved.

CHAPTER 1
FLIGHT OF THE FLAME-BATS

WHILE A pre-dawn hush lay over New York City—
while millions slept unaware that world destiny hung
in the balance—a desperate, secret plan went into operation,
backed by the feverish hope that a great nation might be saved
from doom!

Furtive activity hummed on the great pier where the *Rescuer*
lay anchored in the inky waters of the Hudson River, blanketed
by the blackness of the night. Her decks were dark. Only a dim
glow from the wharf lights shone on the massive freight gangs as
the crew labored. Officers watched the unloading of the precious
cargo with thin-drawn lips and grim eyes. Quickly, quietly, the
work went on as the deadline of dawn approached—ghostly
figures toiling in a phantom ship....

Thousands of miles of sea trail lay behind this mightiest of
ocean freighters. Each turn of her screws had sped her under
full steam along a secret lane from a secret port to this pier in
the greatest city in the United States. She had crept silently into
the Hudson under cover of night, carrying not only her treasure
cargo, but—the fate of a world power!

Weighty boxes rolled down the freight gangs and the sweat-
ing crew wrestled them into ponderous trucks. Out of the hold
came the endless parade of iron-banded crates on which cryptic
marks were blackly stenciled; they were heaved into the trucks,

2

The flame-bats were

dropping thermite bombs!

pile upon pile. Powerful motors snorted; heavy wheels turned as the mysterious freight was moved away. And while the unloading went on at an anxious pace, armed guards stood on watch.

Men in uniform, rifles ready for instant action, completely surrounded the pier. Other uniformed riflemen rode with the cargo as the giant trucks snarled on their way. Still others were stationed strategically in the bleak streets along the route the lorries followed; they signaled all other traffic aside and kept the dark way open. At a point not far distant from the pier, where the Hudson lapped nearby, the trucks were unloaded by still other uniformed men as rapidly as they approached.

Every inch of the journey was amply protected; but here the guards were even thicker. The iron-strapped boxes—small but amazingly heavy to the men who handled them—were carried into a sooty, brick building. There they were piled on the platform of an elevator. The big cage lowered them slowly below street-level. In muffled darkness, still other men transferred the boxes to small, flat-bed cars resting on rusty rails. Dim electric lights illuminated the curving length of a shiny-walled tunnel as the cars shuttled in loaded and came back empty. Efficiently, dextrously, these secret operations were packing the precious cargo of the *Rescuer* into caverns hidden deep beneath the streets of New York City.

In the freighter, the store of boxes diminished; in the tunnels, the stacks of heavy crates mounted. So intent was every man and officer upon his work that none noticed the breathy, fluttering sound hovering in the sky above the Hudson.

Darkness blotted the flitting vanes of a weird craft that hung in the air over the *Rescuer*. No glow of river lights reached up to it. The sound of its muffled motor was a whisper lost in the damp wind sweeping across the busy pier. Like some curious creature of the night, the autogyro descended unseen from the black zenith. From its pit, two pairs of alert eyes peered down intently at the strange operations.

THE TWO passengers of the gyro were using powerful binoculars. One was a young man of clean-cut features, of brisk bearing, stamped with a confident poise beyond his twenty-odd years. The other was a freckle-faced boy, with a broad, humorous mouth and a pugnaciously tilted nose. Their craft poised almost motionless in the air while they lowered their glasses and gazed at each other curiously.

The boy asked: "What does it mean, Jimmy?"

Quietly, his companion answered: "It isn't the first time this has happened, Tim. I spotted a similar operation last week, and I've watched two other big freighters unload since then. The strangest thing about it is—"

"Those men are wearing the uniform of the United States Infantry!" the Irish lad exclaimed. "Those are army trucks!"

The young man nodded. "Yet," he said quietly, "every attempt I've made to find out the meaning of all this has led nowhere. This is undoubtedly work of the army, but the Chief of Staff flatly refused to give me any information about it—while, always before, he has cooperated with me willingly. When I went to the Secretary of War, he declined point-blank to comment on it—and previously he had been friendly and helpful."

"But Z-7?" the boy asked, with some wonder in his voice. "What did he say?"

"Z-7," the young man continued, "had nothing to say—nothing! He evaded my questions. It is certain now that orders have gone to the heads of all government departments to be absolutely silent about these movements." He paused, went on

grimly. "What's more, I know that I have been shadowed—shadowed on the orders of Z-7!" He peered again at the dark deck of the *Rescuer*, his eyes narrowed thoughtfully. "But in spite of all that, I'm going to find out what this means for myself!"

His touch at the controls of the autogyro sent it soaring higher in the clinging darkness. It swooped along the glistening bank of the Hudson, northward toward the point at which the trucks were being unloaded. The double parade of lorries was still underway; the guards in the streets were still alert at their posts. All New York was silent, except this area of odd, frantic activity below.

The young man at the controls of the vaned craft declared with sudden determination: "We are going down to that freighter!"

The freckle-faced lad studied his face intently as the great fans sliced the air again. He brought it to a spot directly above the *Rescuer*. After hovering a moment, he manipulated the controls to plunge the gyro downward. His deft touches sent it directly toward the open after-deck of the huge freighter. And even as he descended, the barely perceptible sighing of his engine aroused startled activity on the deck.

Officers peered upward, snapped sharp orders. Uniformed guards rushed up the gangs and down the companionways, their rifles pointed aloft. The passengers of the gyro watched in cold alarm, but the descent of the craft did not waver. The young man at the controls dropped it gently to the scrubbed deck and, with motor cut, peered around at grim-faced men—and into the black bores of many leveled rifles.

"After me, Tim," he directed quietly, and with calm deliberation, he stepped from the pit.

An officer marched forward stiffly. The young man was startled to see that he was wearing a uniform of the United States Navy and the decorations of a Rear-Admiral. Even more surprised, as the officer stepped closer in the dim glow, he recognized him as a member of the General Staff. The officer paused, and they scrutinized each other in silence.

"You," the young man observed, "are Rear-Admiral Gordon, Director of the War Plans Division, Joint Board of the United States Army and Navy. Good evening, sir!"

"And who," Rear-Admiral Gordon demanded stiffly, "are you?"

THE YOUNG man's answer was to remove a flat silver case from an inner pocket. His thumbnail pressed a concealed spring, and it opened. Inside lay a framed letter. Without releasing the case, the young man extended it so that the naval officer could read:

OPERATOR 5

THE WHITE HOUSE
Washington

To Whom It May Concern:

The identity of the bearer of this letter must be kept strictly confidential.

He is Operator 5 of the United States Intelligence Service.

The signature affixed to the credential was that of the President of the United States.

Rear-Admiral Gordon's brilliant black eyes widened in surprise. He blurted: "I have heard of you, young man. It's a privilege to meet you. I'm well aware that you have rendered exceptional service to your country but—have you special permission to come aboard this vessel?"

"I have not."

"Then I am obliged to order you to leave at once. If it were not for your exemplary record, I would feel obliged to take you prisoner."

The eyes of Operator 5—whose name in the secret archives of the United States Intelligence Service was recorded as James Christopher—narrowed shrewdly. "I have come aboard," he answered quietly, "only to assure myself that this is actually an operation of the army and navy—and not the activity of some subversive organization disguised in our uniforms."

"I am forbidden to give out any information," Rear-Admiral Gordon declared, "but I can assure you that this is indeed an official operation of the government. My orders are for you to leave at once!"

Operator 5 stepped closer. "Admiral Gordon, I am not here to pry into official secrets—though you should know that any such matter would be absolutely safe with me. I'm here to warn you that, whatever this operation is, it's threatened with grave danger."

"What?" Admiral Gordon's eyes sharpened. "How can you know anything whatever about this? Never mind, young man! I cannot discuss the matter with you at all. I have ordered you to leave this ship, and unless you do, I shall be obliged to take forcible measures."

"Are you in highest command here?" Operator 5 asked tightly. "If not, I ask to be taken to the officer in charge at once!"

"I refuse—!"

The quiet of the deck was broken by a strangled cry. It came with such startling suddenness—so without warning—that the words of Admiral Gordon choked in his throat. Operator 5 half-spun into the breeze that had carried the stifled shout—and heard it again! Suddenly, overhead, quick footfalls sounded. They stopped abruptly. An instant later, from below, a resounding splash eddied the water.

Jimmy Christopher started away. He ignored the indignant shout of Admiral Gordon as he darted to the rail. Tim Donovan kept at his side; together they peered down into the heaving black. Churning foam marked where something—or someone—had plunged. Faintly, from the gloom below, came a rhythmic ripple which meant that someone was swimming rapidly.

A heavy hand clamped upon Jimmy Christopher's shoulder

and Admiral Gordon's cold voice began: "I'll make you a prisoner, I warn you, unless you leave—"

"Order that man to be captured!" Jimmy Christopher interrupted quickly. "He'll be out of reach in a minute! Make me prisoner if you like—but I'm not leaving just yet!"

HE SHRUGGED Gordon's hand away, whirled again, and bounded for the ladder. Another snapping command from Gordon sent men plunging after him as he climbed, with Tim Donovan following close behind. He took long, swift strides across the deck toward a door that was standing open, shafting out light. He stepped across the sill, stopped short in amazement.

Blood marked the captain's quarters and the two men in it. One was lying sprawled on the floor, staring with glazed eyes toward the light. His shirt, ripped open, disclosed ghastly crimson stains, still glistening wetly. A knife had been driven hard against his chest, directly over the heart. The second man was kneeling beside the first, one coat-sleeve ripped and red-stained, the arm hanging limp. He straightened in white-faced alarm as Operator 5 exclaimed: "Mr. Secretary!"

The man who peered in terror at Jimmy Christopher was a member of the President's cabinet—the Secretary of War. The man who lay dead at his feet was one of his best-known assistants, a distant relative of the Chief Executive of the nation. Admiral Gordon stopped short behind Operator 5 and Tim Donovan; for a moment, the three of them stared in horror.

Jimmy Christopher snapped across his shoulder: "Get that man who's swimming away!" He stepped into the cabin, unconscious of the infantrymen who had grimly followed him. He stooped over the dead man, realized that the knife had dealt death. Obviously, the same weapon had slashed the Secretary's arm. A bloody footprint, smeared on the floor, marked the way the murderer had hastily fled.

"He—he sprang at me and Layton fought him off!" the Secretary exclaimed. "He meant to kill me, but Layton—"

"Who was he?" Operator 5 asked quickly. "Why did he attack you?"

The Secretary answered breathily: "I—I don't know! Layton and I were in here, discussing the plan for—the plan—" The Cabinet member had checked himself and warily amended his statement. "Layton looked through the window and saw that man—near the rail—signaling. He had a flashlight, pointing upward—and Layton called to him to stop."

"Signaling?" Operator 5 asked quickly. "You're sure of that, sir?"

"Yes—he must've been signaling. He stopped when Layton called. Layton ordered him to come in, and he came to the door. He was an infantryman—or seemed to be—but suddenly he drew a knife and sprang forward. Layton saved me from him—I struck him with a chair just as Layton fell—and he ran away!"

"An infantryman?" Operator 5's eyes darkened. He turned to Admiral Gordon. "Perhaps, after all, sir, not all the men aboard this ship are engaged in official business. You've got to do everything possible to find that killer! I suspected—"

Gordon interrupted with a brittle tone: "I ordered this young man off the ship, Mr. Secretary, and he has refused to go. What has just happened demands that I take him prisoner."

Operator 5 whirled on the Admiral. "Don't you understand that a murderer is escaping—a man who has destroyed one of the directors of the United States? Unless you capture him, the syndicate he is working for may—"

"I am in command here under the Secretary," Admiral Gordon answered with a snap. "I have given the proper orders. My concern is with you. I have strict instructions—"

"Which I hope," Operator 5 interjected, "will be amended now!" He turned urgently to the Secretary, whose face was white with pain. "I am not meddling, sir. I am here for a vitally important reason. I'd like your permission to remain and learn—"

THE SECRETARY blurted: "You are subject to Admiral Gordon's orders! He has declared you a prisoner, and that is final!"

Operator 5's eyes clouded with amazement and chagrin. He stepped closer to the Secretary of War, and his voice became edged.

"Sir, why was this attempt made on your life? Why was the man you saw—the man who tried to kill you—signaling? What is this ship's cargo, and why is it being hidden—and what danger does that signal mean to it? Answer those questions for yourself and you'll realize that instead of holding me prisoner, you should be issuing orders to protect this ship and—"

"From what?" Gordon snapped, almost pettishly.

"From a secret power that has just destroyed a statesman's life and may well destroy the nation!"

Operator 5's statement brought a startled silence in the captain's quarters. Unconsciously, the Secretary peered down at the dead face of his assistant; he straightened wearily. Jimmy Christopher stood alert, listening intently. At his side, Tim Donovan, freckled face blanched, tugged anxiously at the broken bill of his cap.

It was his whisper that broke the tense silence. "Jimmy—do you hear that? It sounds like—!"

A step sounded near the door. The infantrymen guarding it moved aside as a gruff command was spoken. The man who strode into the cabin was garbed entirely in gray. His eyes glittered like black diamonds as he paused, peering at Jimmy Christopher—a grim-faced, poised, commanding figure. At sight of him, Operator 5 exclaimed, "Chief!"

This man, commander of all the undercover activities of the United States Intelligence Service around the globe, was known even to his most trusted lieutenants only as Z-7.

Z-7 stood motionless as Rear-Admiral Gordon's rushing words told about the murder of the Assistant Secretary of War, of Operator 5's stubborn defiance of orders. His dark eyes smouldered and his shoulders hunched as though he were steeling himself to meet a trying demand. As the naval officer finished, he said in his chesty voice: "Admiral Gordon's orders must stand, Operator 5."

"You mean, Chief, that I am to be held a prisoner here?" Jimmy Christopher asked quietly, wonderingly.

"A prisoner—yes! You are in my custody. You will remain with me until this secret mission is completed and until I leave the ship."

Operator 5 answered softly: "Very well, Chief!" His eyes lifted again, and again he listened. At his side, Tim Donovan stood frowning with apprehension. They sensed, rather than heard, an ominous drumming in the air—an irregular throbbing as of airplane exhausts discording together, muffled by great distance. The silence was broken again when a ruddy-faced infantry officer stepped in to report:

"The man who jumped overboard has gotten away, sir. We're still hunting for him, but I'm afraid it's hopeless now."

Z-7's heavy eyebrows shadowed his eyes as he muttered orders that cleared the Captain's quarters. The Secretary of War, wincing with the pain of his slashed arm, was hurried away for first aid. Rear-Admiral Gordon closed the cabin, turned the key in the lock. Z-7, head bowed in thought, went quietly to the rail; and Jimmy Christopher, with Tim Donovan, followed.

"Chief," he observed with quiet bitterness, "the mission of this ship has become known to some power hostile to the United States—and yet it is being kept secret from me."

Z-7 ANSWERED quietly. "I must remind you again, Operator 5, that the Secretary of State is now the supreme head of the Intelligence. I am absolutely under his orders. In this case, the Cabinet is acting as a unit, to coördinate all defense departments of the government. It is a situation demanding the closest possible secrecy. Only a very few Intelligence men know the meaning of this strategy—by order of the Secretary of State."

"Chief, I cannot question the decisions of my superiors," Operator 5 mused quietly, "but I should like to know, if I may, why I have been excluded from those who know the meaning of this mission."

Z-7 hesitated before he answered: "Those reasons, I am sorry to say, I cannot divulge."

Operator 5 tightened. "You can't tell me, Chief?" he asked quickly. "Why not?"

Z-7's dark eyes glittered darkly as he answered. "A month ago, when the Intelligence was made a unit under the Department of State, the Secretary discharged half our men and imposed a rigid Code of Intelligence on us under which we are bound to conduct our investigations. We became understaffed and handicapped at every turn, under the orders of a man who unfortunately understands nothing whatsoever of intelligence work. It was at that time that an unlawful organization sprang up which called itself the Hidden Hundred."

Quietly Jimmy Christopher added: "Composed, it's believed, of ex-Intelligence men who continue to serve their country in spite of the Secretary's hamstringing regulations."

"Men who," Z-7 corrected grimly, "regardless of their motives and their results, are acting illegally. They have defied me and the Secretary. They have offered a challenge which the Secretary has chosen to meet. I have standing orders to destroy the Hidden

Hundred and to capture their leader. It is my duty to do so, and I intend to fulfill that duty. Once I unmask that man, once I find evidence to convict him before a court-martial, the penalty for his leadership of the Hidden Hundred must be—death!"

Deeper darkness came into Operator 5's blue eyes.

"You ask why you have not been admitted to the secret of

A blinding flash of flame appeared. White-hot
blazes spread swift havoc over the freighter's deck!

this government mission," Z-7 continued levelly. "Perhaps the
answer lies in what I have just told you."

Operator 5's eyes searched Z-7's.

The chief of the United States Intelligence went on, speaking

17

very low: "My boy, you're the most valuable agent in the Intelligence. You have rendered far greater service to your country than any other operator who has ever lived. It isn't only that, but—well you're as dear to me as though you were my own son. Will you always remember that?"

The Washington chief straightened tensely. "There is no evidence now pointing to the identity of the captain of the Hidden Hundred, Operator 5. There is only a suspicion—but it is becoming a conviction in the mind of the Secretary of State. If strong evidence ever comes to hand, it must be acted upon. I cannot avoid that, much as I might wish to. I can do nothing but follow the orders of my superior—and doom that man to death!"

Jimmy Christopher stood motionless, his breath coming slowly, burning through his dry throat. Tim Donovan, wide-eyed at his side, searched Z-7's grim face. The Washington chief, tight-nerved, eyes shining with agony, confronted Operator 5 a long, silent moment.

"Good God, my boy!" he blurted. "Have you nothing to say?"

Operator 5's dry lips parted to speak—but his words were silenced by a sudden blaze of light, by a muffled concussion that surged across the black water, by a flare of flames that sprang high into the sky like a signal of doom.

Jimmy Christopher whirled. Peering across the rail, his eyes reflected the gleam of the leaping fire. Hundreds of yards away, fluttering like a gigantic torch in the wind, flames sprang blindingly. Hoarse shouts of dismay carried across the water, mingling with an ominous drumming that had become lost to

Jimmy Christopher's ears during the Chief's grave words—a sound that now sent his blood coursing hotly.

"Planes!" he exclaimed. "They're above the spot where the trucks are unloading! More of them—directly overhead!"

AGAIN MUFFLED explosions boomed across the water, drumming into the hush of the coming dawn. As the concussions broke, fresh flames leaped skyward. The glitter of the blaze shone on swooping wings far overhead—wings black as the zenith above them. The glistening shone on the sweeping bats of doom as Jimmy Christopher whirled and sped across the deck.

He was about to bound down the companionway, to the deck where his autogyro sat, when Z-7's hard hand gripped his arm. "Operator 5! You are a prisoner aboard this ship—in my custody! You must stay here!"

"Stay?" Jimmy Christopher snapped the word as he turned back. "No man must stay on this ship! Order them off, Z-7! Those planes are dropping bombs—incendiary bombs! Listen to them directly above! Order this ship abandoned now—before it's too late!"

Z-7 peered up, glimpsed the ominous flicker of black wings, heard the muffled droning; but his hand remained tight on Jimmy Christopher's arm. "I'll give those orders now—but you're to remain with me, Operator 5!"

"I'm going up, Chief! I've got to spot those planes and—"

A sharp, whistling sound pierced the air above the *Rescuer*. It grew louder swiftly; and suddenly a drumming concussion rolled across the deck. It was a deadened, hollow sound, totally unlike the bursting of a high-explosive charge; but it spread swift havoc. At the stem of the freighter, a blinding splash of fire appeared. White-hot stuff flew. Sizzling with a vicious hiss, it spewed across the deck. Wherever it touched, flames sprang up instantly.

With a desperate twist, Jimmy Christopher tore himself from Z-7's grasp. The Washington chief groped to stop him, but he sped down the ladder with Tim Donovan at his heels. Z-7's voice rang out! "Abandon ship!" Through the crackling of the fire Operator 5 leaped toward the gyro. He sprang after the Irish lad into the pit; he cranked the motor into action; he thrust the throttle wide, staring into the spreading blaze.

Swiftly the vaned craft leaped off the deck, rising almost vertically in the shine of the flames. Jimmy Christopher peered down, appalled to see great gaping holes appearing in the deck of the *Rescuer* with fire gushing up. He swung swiftly up the Hudson River, his startled gaze upon a howling mass of flames at the point where the United States trucks had discharged their mysterious cargo.

As he swung closer, he saw great sections of pavement heave up from the streets, saw huge geysers of blue fire leap from broken gas-mains—saw the spread of swift destruction!

CHAPTER 2
MASK OF GOLD

HOSTILE AIRCRAFT, swooping furtively out of the night sky, were raining havoc into the streets of the slumbering metropolis!

20

Operator 5 brought his neat automatic into his hand as he soared high in the darkness. Tim Donovan gripped the cowling beside him, stunned by sight of the destruction spreading below. Through the flickering of the flames, black-vaned bombs streaked downward. Each struck with a dull concussion, spattering white-hot stuff that unleashed a contagion of flame all around it. The fire spread swiftly to the very edge of the river, into the crisscrossing of streets, striking terror in its wake.

Around the blue plumes which leaped from the burst gas-mains, men ran madly, their uniforms ablaze. Others lay motionless on the broken pavement, dead amid the volcanic holocaust. Trucks were lumbering away from the stricken area like lumbering, stampeding elephants. Some lay trapped in the great gaping holes in the streets; some had run wild and crashed headlong into buildings; others blazed even as they fled. The street gleamed with the white heat of a raging inferno.

Beneath Operator 5, blinding light flared; above him flitted the wings of the attacking flame-bats. He manipulated the controls of his gyro to climb swiftly. He and the boy, Tim, were alone; his only weapon was his automatic—to attempt to repulse the attack singlehanded was hopeless. Rising so that he might follow the sky-trail of the winged spreaders of havoc, he watched them swoop down to their marks, drop their vaned projectiles of destruction, and soar again.

"Autogyros—like this one, Jimmy!" Tim Donovan exclaimed breathlessly. "No marks on them—all black!"

"Outlaw crates, Tim!" Operator 5 agreed quickly. "Watch them, old-timer, and warn me if one spots us!"

The vaned craft which lifted Jimmy Christopher high into the zenith was his own. His undercover work for the Intelligence demanded swift transportation to all parts of the nation, and he kept this gyro hangared in a hidden spot on Manhattan for use in case of emergencies. And now an entire fleet of similar craft had been secreted in or near the city by a hostile power that was striking with the coming of dawn—a mysterious attack upon a still more mysterious mission of the United States Government!

Operator 5 exclaimed: "Thermite bombs, Tim! The stuff burns its way through everything it touches!* The *Rescuer* is sinking now!"

THE GREAT freighter was listing at the pier. From stem

---

* AUTHOR'S NOTE: Thermite, a mixture of aluminum powder and iron oxide, is used commercially for welding and for extracting metals from ore—but it is also a highly destructive weapon of war. When this mixture is ignited by a bit of ordinary magnesium ribbon, it burns with a temperature of between 2,300 and 2,700 degrees Centigrade. The burning powder, when dropped in a bomb and scattered by a mild bursting charge, becomes a terrifying spreader of havoc.

In the official magazine of the German army, Lieut.-General Altrock describes the effect of electric incendiary bombs which weigh only one kilogram (approximately two pounds):

"They have only to strike through a roof, and then the thermite with which they are filled develops a heat of almost 3,000 degrees; the outer covering also burns, and this glowing mass can eat its way through steel. Water merely increases the incendiary effect, and no extinguishing appliance has yet been discovered. The destructive and incendiary effect will also be felt in the to stern, high flames enveloped it, rising from the depths of her hull. The thermite bombs had turned her plates to molten steel. The black water of the Hudson was rushing into her; before many minutes she would lie on the bottom. And over her the black bats still hovered like birds of prey.

"Whatever the *Rescuer's* cargo was, Tim," Jimmy Christopher muttered grimly, "it's destroyed now!"

In the sky, the bat-like craft were swinging together into a formation. Their muffled exhausts beat an ominous thunder into the night as they flocked up the river. Operator 5, watching them intently, nudged his controls to soar after them, to keep close enough that he would not lose them in the thick darkness. The light of the flames grew dimmer on their black wings as they sped away from the disaster they had wrought.

A glance backward told Jimmy Christopher that fire-fighting units were speeding to fight the howling fire. Down the avenues and the cross-streets, engines were rushing, sirens screaming,

streets. Flames as high as houses will burst forth from the gas mains which are laid along the streets and the population will be in a state of utter panic." Ludendorff, former Field-Marshal of the German Army, expressed a similar view in his memoirs concerning the effects of electric incendiary bombs. According to him, important preparations were being made in 1918 to set fire to London and Paris by air bombs, which were to be filled with thermite. No one, therefore, can doubt the truth of the assertion made by Lieut. Siegert, Inspector of the German Air Fleet, in the *Berliner Illtistrierte Zeitung*, that a few airplanes dropping thermite bombs will be able to reduce the capital of any great state to ashes.

rubber-coated men clinging to their sides. Everywhere else, the city still lay gloomy and quiet and dark while here the torch of secret war flared high in the heavens.

Cautiously, Operator 5 swung his gyro above the black ribbon of the Hudson, straining his eyes to keep the flitting bats of doom in sight. Tim Donovan, alert at his side, searched the air all around. The dull droning of the many exhausts was a baffling constant sound; yet through it, the Irish lad sensed a threat of danger. His hand shot hard to Operator 5's arm and he warned:

"One of them is coming close, Jimmy! I can't see it, but it's not with the others and it's—"

A flash of gunfire in the sky, the sharp crack of a report, broke into the boy's words—and a bullet whistled past Operator 5's head!

He twisted swiftly, swinging his automatic. Above and behind him, like a vulture pouncing on unsuspecting prey, one of the vaned craft was plummeting swiftly. Above its pit, the head and shoulders of a man were outlined dimly against the sky. He was raising a weapon to his shoulder and Operator 5 glimpsed the outlines of a submachine gun. His finger tightened on the trigger of his automatic as the very instant a stuttering burst broke from the powerful weapon.

Slugs slashed across the wings of Jimmy Christopher's crate as he thrust at the controls and swerved. A full surge of power from his motor sent him spinning higher—but the muzzle of the submachine gun followed him. Tim Donovan's tough hands gripped the controls while Operator 5 turned to face the threat. His automatic blazed swiftly three times. His parading bullets were still buzzing through the air when the other weapon coughed again.

Its slugs slapped through the cockpit behind Operator 5. Again it sent out a burst of slugs that screamed high into the sky. Grimly watching, while Tim Donovan swerved the gyro swiftly away, Jimmy Christopher saw the black pilot heave back—and knew that his counterattack had told. He watched the other plane poise, stagger a moment, then dart like a dragonfly. He grasped the controls from Tim's hands and swung swiftly to follow.

IN THE distant night, high above the Hudson, the other crates were whisking out of hearing now. Operator 5, chancing to lose the trail in the black depths of the air, chose quickly to follow the flame-bat which had struck at him. It wavered in the air, swooped, recovered, darted, slowed. Its erratic movements revealed clearly that the wounded pilot was striving fruitlessly to rejoin the fleeing black bevy—but its only certain direction was downward.

Operator 5 followed grimly as it fluttered toward the eastern bank of the river at a point far north of the center of attack. The pilot's head appeared over the cowling, lolling above hunched shoulders; he peered down, seeking a landing. The crate swooped again, toward the flat blackness of an open pier near upper Riverside Drive. Once around it, Jimmy Christopher circled while it sagged again. Then its trucks bounced against the splintered wood of the pier; it rolled a few feet; and its vanes drooped as it poised motionless.

Gently, warily, Jimmy Christopher brought his own craft down behind it. Automatic in hand, he legged over the cowling. Tim Donovan whispered a warning as he walked slowly, directly, to the other crate. Far below, on the river, the glare of the fire shone, but there was no other light. In the distance, flames were roaring dully; but there was no other sound. Operator 5 raised himself, peered into the pit at a still figure huddled almost on the floor of the cockpit.

Tim Donovan heard him say quietly as he stepped down again: "Dead!"

Quickly Operator 5 inspected the gyro. Its black paint covered any possible identification number or mark. He climbed into the pit, and with the aid of Tim Donovan, extricated the lifeless pilot. He touched the button of his electric torch, and its gleam shone in the white, placid face. Tim heard Operator 5 mutter a name: "Wanvig!" He rose, and his hand strayed unconsciously to a little golden ornament dangling on his watch-chain.

It was a delicately carved skull-and-crossbones, its eyes glittering ruby red—a symbol of death.

Suddenly he moved, began stripping out of his perfectly tailored suit. Tim Donovan watched anxiously while he removed the uniform from the dead man—a uniform as black, as unmarked, as the craft he had flown. He pulled himself into it, tightened his belt, buttoned the tunic, ran his hands through

26

his pockets. He brought from one of them a strip of velvet in which eyeholes were cut—a mask.

"Come, Tim!" he called.

Together they carried the dead man to the other gyro, and lifted him over the cowling. Operator 5 left the crate locked as he returned to the black ship. He signaled Tim Donovan up; climbed to the controls. He started the motor, and through the muffled surge of power the Irish lad asked anxiously:

"Jimmy! What're you going to do?"

"I'm going to find out what this means, Tim," Operator 5 answered tensely. "I'm going to get at the bottom of this double secret!"

The singing motor rolled the gyro along the pier a few yards; Operator 5's touch on the controls sent it climbing steeply into the air. As it swept out across the black water of the Hudson, he opened the engine to its full power. Flitting like a huge bat, it followed the course of the river while Jimmy Christopher strained his ears to pick up the throbbing exhaust of the other craft.

Had they already landed? Had they already outdistanced him? Was the air trail lost? The questions were soon answered, and a bursting sigh of relief came from Jimmy Christopher's lungs. He sensed a faint vibration in the air....

HE SOARED as he searched, and as he followed the black curve of the river past the high Palisades, he glimpsed the faint flutter of revolving vanes and spinning props. With the utmost caution, he pulled over to the bevy of bats. The darkness sheltered him as he dropped slowly toward them. In a moment, he was flying through the night at the edge of the strange flock of havoc-bringers.

"Down, Tim!" he warned. "Keep out of sight!"

He peered at the strange craft coursing with him through the blackness. He saw pilots huddled in the cowlings—men who glanced about in every direction warily, constantly alert for pursuit. He matched their speed as they swung away from the river and headed over rugged territory. His nerves tightened as he sensed that the black flock was nearing its destination.

The next moment confirmed his hunch and quickened his pulse. The leader of the bat formation swooped groundward. Operator 5 could glimpse no beacon in the dark territory below, but the other craft followed the leader with confidence. Jimmy Christopher deduced that an infrared beam, discernible only through special equipment in the leader's craft, was marking a hidden field below.

He peered around quickly as he groped into the pit. An exclamation of satisfaction passed his lips when he touched the metal cabinet of a shortwave wireless installation. He clicked the switch, and a green glow shone from the dials. Carefully he trimmed the oscillator of the transmitter, fitted phones to his ears, brought a microphone close to his lips. Crackling static faded away and he spoke crisply:

"Calling MR! Operator 5 calling MR, no distorter!"

He realized that this move entailed great risk—that receivers in the other planes, or on the field below, might be picking up his voice. His very call to the Intelligence headquarters concealed on Manhattan was a betrayal of his identity and presence. Yet he chanced the danger and repeated tersely: "Calling MR! Operator 5 calling MR and Z-7—*urgent!*"

A voice spoke briskly out of the ether. "MR on the wave. We've got you, Operator 5, but Z-7 is not here. Have you a report?"

Jimmy Christopher answered briskly: "I am in one of the gyros which attacked the *Rescuer* a short while ago. We have proceeded to a hidden field west of the Hudson, within the Bear Mountain region. Please flash Mitchell Field if you cannot reach Z-7, and hold yourself ready for further reports."

"Waiting on this band, Operator 5!"

Around Jimmy Christopher, the bats were plunging to the ground. They descended with a confidence that meant each pilot knew this field even in total darkness. Operator 5 plied his controls gingerly, peering down at black ground blurring toward him. His trucks touched; he cut the motor. Almost a score of gyros were roosting on a flat, open field. Operator 5 stooped to whisper to the anxious Irish boy crouching beneath the cowling:

"Wait here, Tim. Eyes and ears open! In case of an emergency, you must get as full a report as possible back to Z-7. Understand, old-timer?"

The boy asked with hushed anxiety: "What about you, Jimmy?"

"I'm going with these other pilots. It's a chance, but it must be taken. Remember, Tim, if anything breaks, you're to get into the air and away from here. Never mind me, old-timer—but get that report back to the Chief. That's orders."

"Gee, Jimmy!" the boy protested; then: "Okay—I'll get that report back."

"Good boy, Tim!"

OPERATOR 5'S lips curved in a tight smile of admiration as he climbed from the pit. Tim Donovan was too young to be included in the roster of accredited Intelligence agents, but Jimmy Christopher considered him the equal of any man in the service. Tim's uncanny ability to shadow had served Operator 5 well in a dozen vital cases in the past. Since the stormy night when, hungry and homeless, the little Irish lad had saved Operator 5 from a gangster's bullet, they had been inseparable co-workers in the cause of the Service.

The ring worn by Tim Donovan—a white skull blazoned against a black background, with the mystic numeral 5 on its forehead—picturing Operator 5's watch-charm—was a sign by which all Intelligence agents could recognize him as Jimmy Christopher's unofficial assistant.

Operator 5 turned, peered at the shadowy figures of the pilots leaving their weird craft. Quietly, with firm step, he followed them as they gathered. He noted that each of them was masked; quickly he drew the strip of velvet across his eyes and fastened it. He strode with the black-uniformed men across the field. A huge house loomed out of the darkness. No light shone from it; it appeared to be deserted; yet there was an air of tense activity pervading this secret field.

Suddenly every man became motionless. Masked eyes turned upward while a droning sound came out of the heavens. It grew louder each moment; and in the sky, colored beacons appeared like constellations of stars.  Slowly the bright points of light drifted across the zenith, marking the flight of a formation of planes. No man moved. They suspected a fact which Operator 5 knew to be true: these were United States army crates from Mitchell Field searching for the flame-bats.

Slowly the planes drifted out of sight beyond the rugged hills—their mark missed. Operator 5 heard a mutter from the pilots as they formed a line at a broad door of the house. He took his position with them, noting that each placed himself several feet away from the man ahead and the man behind. Slowly the file moved forward as the big door of the house opened and closed.

Operator 5 heard signals exchanged, passwords whispered. Coldness came to his heart as the file of men neared the door. He tried to hear the words spoken by the masked pilot directly ahead of him. At the black door, he heard a whispered question and the muffled answer: "Midas." The entrance opened and closed again. Operator 5 faced the guard, next in line.

"The password?" the question came out of the gloom.

"Midas."

"Your number?"

The coldness tightened around Operator 5's heart as he was forced to risk a guess: "Five."

"Enter."

He stepped into blackness with icy misgivings filling him.

He walked along a corridor as though he had entered this house many times and knew exactly what was expected of him. He noted heavy drapes in an arch fluttering as though they had just been parted, boldly stepped through. He found himself in a dimly lighted room where the other masked pilots were waiting. He took his position among them.

BEHIND HIM, three other masked and uniformed men entered. An expectant hush fell. At last, a faint rustling turned all eyes toward weighty portières at the far side of the room. They parted, and a man stepped into the light. Sight of him sent a shock of baffled surprise through Operator 5.

The face of this man was masked in gold. Golden mesh, fashioned of such minute links that it shone like satin, it framed the wearer's whitish eyes. A gold-bearded border extended across this man's forehead and full cheeks. So bright was the sheen of the mask that it covered the man's entire face with a golden haze of light, in which only the startling white eyes shone clearly.

Every man in the room snapped a salute to the wearer of the gold mask. He made no gesture in return; his gaze was in itself an answer. Operator 5 felt, as he gazed at this dominating figure, an uncanny power, as though the gold-masked man deemed no strength greater than his own—not even the force of death. His presence commanded utter silence; he gazed upon the pilots with eyes sparkling like ice.

"Well done, gentlemen! Splendid!"

His tone had a hollow, resonant quality. Operator 5's impression—startling even to himself—was that this was a voice speaking from another world—a sepulchral voice that might reach even beyond the limits of death....

"Well done!" The man in the gold mask moved to face the pilots. Their eyes shifted to follow him; otherwise they did not move. His gaze upon them was again an imperious command.

"Our work," he said in his strange, muffled tones, "has begun auspiciously indeed. We have utterly destroyed a vital military store of the United States. Each step we take now will render the United States still weaker in armament—yet that, as you know, is not our whole purpose. We will strike our telling blow—a blow that will topple the United States from its very foundations—not with a weapon of steel—but with a weapon of gold!"

Silence—while Operator 5 studied the cold, white eyes of the man in the golden mask.

"We have already discussed in detail," the sepulchral voice continued, "each successive step of our master plan. We proceed without hesitancy. Tomorrow night we strike another staggering blow in Washington. Night after next we will destroy the great plant which is now working night and day to provide the United States Government with stores of ammunition and munitions. Midnight is our zero hour, when we take our mighty steps toward triumph."

A chill coursed through Jimmy Christopher's veins as he realized the startling import of this cold, calmly spoken pronouncement of doom.

"Tonight our master strategy is underway, and I step temporarily from the command. A move of which even you do not know demands my supervision. During my absence, you will receive your orders from my first lieutenant. You will, gentlemen, obey implicitly any communication signed with the name of Haigh."

The name shot a fresh chill through Operator 5's heart—for it was that of the most influential Ambassador in Washington, the representative of a European power engaged even now in a ruthless financial war with the United States.

"I extend to you my congratulations upon a night's work well done, gentlemen, and I bid you adieu until—"

THE MAN in the gold mask broke off as the heavy drapes rustled. Through them, another man stepped—masked, like the pilots, in black. He stared at the black-masked faces, advanced quickly to the speaker, proffered a slip of paper and stood breathless until the white eyes of the leader of the secret cabal raised, glittering with deep fires.

JIMMY CHRISTOPHER

"You are dismissed," he said in his ghostly tones, "except Number Five. For him there are special orders."

Operator 5's heart speeded with dread. That was the number he had given at the entrance of this hidden house. He stood motionless, uncertain and anxious, as the other masked men turned smartly and filed from the room. The man in the gold mask stared at him until he stood alone. Abruptly, the white-eyed man turned and strode through the curtains. The other, speaking haltingly, bade Operator 5 with a snap: "Follow!"

Jimmy Christopher's lips pressed grimly as he moved to obey. He sensed danger; yet he was obliged to continue to play his part, for any other move meant immediate self-betrayal. He parted the curtains and stepped through; he followed a thick-carpeted hallway to a carved door. The black-masked man opened it for him, and he entered a sumptuous study filled with a golden light.

Behind a desk stood the man in the golden mask, his eyes of ice fixed immovably on Operator 5. Jimmy Christopher stepped forward, noting with astonishment that all the walls of the room were covered with gold leaf, that all the light fixtures glittered gold, that even the desk set was fashioned of the same precious metal. He faced the desk with squared shoulders, his gaze unwavering on the white eyes.

"Special orders, sir?"

"Yes. Remove your mask."

Again Jimmy Christopher's heart spurted with anxiety; but again he was forced to comply. He unfastened the strip of black velvet and dropped it. His searching gaze caught no flicker of surprise in the masked man's white eyes. The hollow voice came quietly:

"Rather than special orders to execute, there is a special decision you must make. It is this: how do you choose to die?"

Operator 5's squared shoulders settled more firmly. A faint, wry curve came to his lips. He asked quietly: "You wish me to decide now, sir?"

"Now." The massive hand of the man in the golden mask reached inside his coat. It reappeared with a slow, gliding motion—gripping a revolver. Operator 5 felt cold astonishment when he saw that the weapon was of gold. It leveled directly at his heart as the masked man said: "This, I may suggest, is an excellent way. The bullets, you may be interested to know, are of virgin gold."

Tightly Operator 5 answered: "Gold, to you, sir, a weapon signifying destruction—but I prefer steel."

The white eyes flashed angrily. "This is not a game! You will learn that very quickly—when my finger pulls this trigger. Do not add the mistake of challenging me to the mistake you have already made. The password of Number Five, you see, is not Midas, but Sutter Fort."

"Perhaps we both have made mistakes," Operator 5 answered levelly. "You, sir, in thinking your master plan, your strategy, can succeed in weakening the United States—"

"Weaken it?" The words spat from the gold-lighted mouth with bitter vehemence, with deep-felt wrath. "It will crush this contemptible nation out of existence!"

OPERATOR 5'S hand rose slowly to the front of the black tunic that he had removed from a dead man. "You have given me the choice," he said, "of a manner of dying. My decision is made. It is to die with you, sir!"

His swift, supple fingers closed hard on the buckle of the belt he wore beneath his tunic. A sharp flick of his arm jerked it from the loops, sent it flying. A long, narrow sheath, it disclosed a glittering rapier which had been curled around Operator 5's waist. As the metal glinted, a flash of white fire darted in the golden light—from the revolver in the masked man's hand.

The golden bullet snipped at the sleeve of Jimmy Christopher's tunic as he sprang aside. The keen edge of his blade whipped downward with lightning rapidity. It struck once, and the swiftness of the move made the steel a glittering blur. Its touch brought a spurt of red across the hand gripping the golden gun; a wrathful oath burst from the lips of the man in the golden mask. Jimmy Christopher lashed with the blade again and sprang forward.

Numbness paralyzed the hand gripping the plated weapon. Operator 5's blow had cut deep into tendons, striking the gun loose. He gripped the golden weapon as he sprang forward; he whirled away with it in his hands. The man in the golden mask backed with terror glinting in his white eyes. Operator 5's rapier poised above his heart as he stood braced against the wall.

Quickly Jimmy Christopher reached to the desk lamp, and unscrewed the hot bulb. Dropping it aside, he lifted the golden letter-opener from the blotter on the desk. The white eyes followed his moves; the lips which were lighted with the color of gold snarled: "You'll never leave this place alive!"

"Perhaps!"

The man in the golden mask replied with a sudden, ringing shout—a warning and an order to his lieutenants beyond the closed door. The response was immediate—the sound of running feet. As they neared the library, Operator 5 thrust the golden letter-opener into the lamp socket.

A spitting blue spark leaped. The shorted line instantly exploded a fuse. Darkness filled the room in a flash.

Jimmy Christopher whirled. He slipped the golden revolver into his tunic pocket; he gripped up the desk chair. One swing sent it twirling at the broad, curtained windows at the side of the room. Glass crashed and flew. Operator 5 leaped toward the opening.

In the library, hollow, snarling commands rang from the lips of the man in the golden mask. Men came rushing through the black room after Operator 5. As he crouched to dart across the grounds, he glimpsed quick-moving black figures in the darkness. They were springing from all sides, crowding to cut off every path of escape. Operator 5's automatic poised to fire as a vicious gun attack came out of the night.

Flying lead sang a song of death as the ring of masked men closed in on Jimmy Christopher.

CHAPTER 3
SOLDIERS OF SECRECY

DARKNESS SHELTERED Tim Donovan as he crouched in the pit of the black gyro that sat on the hidden field. He had anxiously watched Operator 5 mingle with the masked pilots and enter the house. He had watched the lightless windows of the secret dwelling while Jimmy Christopher's orders echoed in his mind: "In case of emergency, above all get a report back to Z-7." Now he jerked up, startled, as the cracking reports of guns carried across the field.

He saw the flame flashing near the side of the house, saw black men crowding upon a shadow figure that crouched near the wall. He poised in the pit, in an agony of uncertainty, his small hands gripping the cowling. "Jimmy!" he blurted, and suddenly he clambered out.

The Irish lad twisted the crank of the motor desperately. Another turn, with the contact made, and the hot engine caught. Its muffled roar surged across the field as Tim Donovan clambered to the controls. Peering intently through the windshield, he sent the weird craft scurrying across the field—directly toward the spot where the black-uniformed men were crowding.

He glimpsed other forms running toward him, but he gave them scarcely a glance. From scattered points on the field gun-flame flashed—fire licking from the weapons of sentries. The slugs whistled shrilly past the plucky lad's head, but he was thinking only of Operator 5. He sent the vaned crate swooping toward the wall where Jimmy Christopher was crouching with murderous guns turned upon him.

The savage sweep of the wings, the dangerous slashing of the propeller forced the black-uniformed men to retreat. The boy lowered the autogyro. Slugs whipped across the pit as he veered perilously close to the wall. "Jimmy!" broke from his lips, and through the surge of the motor he heard a strained, answering call: "Tim! Hold it!"

The boy clamped the brakes hard, eased the throttle while countless men began running toward him. Operator 5 bounded from the wall of the house. Tim Donovan opened the throttle again as Jimmy Christopher's hands gripped the cowling. Swiftly as the foils could bite the air, he lifted the crate into a steep ascent. Operator 5 tumbled into the pit as the boy swooped the gyro high above the house.

Bullets whined past him, clipping through the wings, raking past the pit. A glance downward showed black figures racing toward the other craft. Through the muffled drumming of the motor, he heard a bellowed command, though no word was distinguishable. Thinking only of losing himself in the blackness of the sky before pursuit could be launched from the hidden field, he opened the engine up wide in a darting flight toward the river.

"Jimmy!" he shouted as the wind howled past. The answer came feebly: "Okay—Tim! Thanks—old-timer!" In dismay the boy twisted, his hand seeking Operator 5's. He felt the stickiness of blood. Jimmy Christopher's white face was streaked with crimson from a wound across his forehead. His eyes were dimmed, rolling with the shock of the bullet. He managed a sigh: "Good boy, Tim—take it away!" But he did not rise.

A TURMOIL of anxiety for Jimmy Christopher filled the tough lad as he sent the gyro skirting southward along the black Hudson. He sensed a vibration in the air behind him, and judged that the other crates had leaped into the pursuit. Carefully, he swung the gyro low, until it hovered close to the water and floated in the shadows of the Palisades. There, while it poised in the air, he turned again to Operator 5.

"Jimmy! You're hurt!"

"Not bad—Tim." The voice was stronger now. "Careful! They'll shoot us down if they spot us."

The warning turned Tim again to the controls; he sent the crate zigzagging swiftly across the dark water. Behind him, the hollow droning of the other gyros grew louder. Cold bewilderment filled him as he reached the point where the Palisades became lost in the lower banks. Abruptly the drumming motor-sounds vanished behind him; the night was still. To the puzzled boy it seemed that the other craft had vanished in mid air....

Through the still night, he kept the gyro coursing along the river. Operator 5 brought himself up painfully. He mopped at the stinging gash cut by a bullet, peered around dazedly. Below, on the fringe of Manhattan, clouds of smoke were still pouring up. The conflagration spread by the flame-bats had been brought under control, but the attacked area was smouldering. Tim Donovan nudged the controls, about to swing the gyro across Manhattan toward its secret hangar, when Operator 5 touched his arm.

"Listen, Tim!"

Out of the quiet of the sky came the humming of a lone, black ship on the prowl. Again, alertly, the Irish lad dropped Jimmy Christopher's craft low to the water. They saw the ghostly wings of the other crate whirling above. The first faint glow of dawn was blending across the sky, silhouetting the other gyro. At top speed, it was flying toward the Bay—and an unusual marking on its wings caught Operator 5's attention.

It was a spot of gold!

To Jimmy Christopher, the disc insignia—a symbol like a

gold coin—meant that this was undoubtedly the craft of the masked leader of the flame-bats. Painfully, he shifted to take the controls as it flitted past. He allowed it to flash ahead; then he followed, matched its speed. Down past the gray turrets of lower Manhattan the chase went—out across the black bay. Operator 5 followed stubbornly while the shoreline receded, while open sea spread ahead....

ABRUPTLY, THE gold-marked gyro dropped, and Jimmy Christopher spotted its destination. On the swells of the outer bay, on water glistening iridescently with the first light of the dawn, a steamer was riding. The gyro with the golden insignia dropped toward the side of it. Its floats swung down; it came to rest on the waves. And from the side of the steamer, a small boat put out.

Flashing oars pulled the boat toward the bobbing craft. Out of its pit, a big man crawled—a man who could be no other than the master of the golden mask. Immediately, the boat turned back. The huge man climbed nimbly up an accommodation ladder; he crossed the steamer deck and was lost from sight. The gold-marked gyro leaped from the water, whirled high, soared northward again.

Operator 5 watched it vanish in the haze of the coming day. Carefully, he directed his own craft toward the steamer. He dropped low, circling it, and noted its name: *Monte Cristo*. Again he sent his craft high into the sky; and as he soared, he touched the switch and the dials of the shortwave wireless apparatus in the pit.

"Calling MR! Operator 5 calling MR and Z-7, no distorter. Can you hear me, MR?"

A crackling answer came: "MR on your wave! Z-7 is coming to the microphone! Stand by!"

A moment later, the chesty voice of the commander-in-chief of the United States Intelligence carried over the ether. "Z-7 speaking. Where are you, Operator 5? What is your report?"

"Chief, I have spotted the man who directed the attack tonight. He has just boarded a steamer in the Bay which is going to sea. It is the *Monte Cristo*. That man may be taken into custody simply by—"

"What?" Z-7's voice interrupted. "What is the name of that ship, Operator 5?"

"The *Monte Cristo*, Chief. That man is the leader of a dangerous espionage ring, but he may be taken off that boat now and his organization broken up if—"

"Orders, Operator 5!" Z-7's crackle came again. "You are to abandon your investigation of the *Monte Cristo* at once! You are to report to me at WDC-13 immediately!"

Operator 5 blinked, with the pain of his wound, with stunned astonishment at the chief's orders. He asked breathily: "Don't you understand, Chief? That man—"

"Abandon the investigation! Report to WDC-13!"

Operator 5 straightened in dismay. Sudden quietness on the wave-band meant that MR had switched off the air. Z-7 had spoken with cold finality. Jimmy Christopher peered mystified at the fog-wreathed outlines of the steamer below. With lips pressed together grimly, he swung his autogyro back toward New York....

IN COMPANY with Tim Donovan, Operator 5 passed through the secret portals of WDC-13. A hidden elevator carried them to the level of the suite of windowless rooms which served as the central headquarters of the United States Intelligence. So cunningly protected was this undercover office that lifelong residents of the Capital might never suspect its existence.

From this point, Z-7 directed the activities of Intelligence agents all over the world; to this point, their reports flashed at all hours of the day and night by cable, teletype, telephone and radio. It was the nerve-center of America's undercover system.

Jimmy Christopher strode directly into an office walled with file cabinets—Z-7's. He found no one at the desk. Anxiously he turned back, and with Tim Donovan walked along a corridor to one of a series of doors. Inside the room beyond, men in smocks were consulting a vast bank of card-index files. Operator 5 took one of the tables, and from his pocket he removed the golden gun of the man in the golden mask.

Tim watched him intently as he worked to develop any latent fingerprints on it. This room contained all known equipment for the process; its collection of prints was the greatest in the world, exceeding even that of the Division of Investigation of the Department of Justice. The science of fingerprints had reached its greatest development in this room, under Z-7's direction; and now Jimmy Christopher made use of its resources.

Black powder of a secret composition, dusted upon the golden gun, made visible a number of clearly defined impressions.

Operator 5 recognized some of them as his own. The others must be those of the wearer of the golden mask. Expertly he photographed them with special apparatus devised for the purpose. The efficient system of the fingerprint division placed clear reproductions of the ridge impressions at his disposal within a few minutes. He wrote the cryptic classification on a card, immediately consulted the bank of files.

His hunt through the "current" section brought no result. The special section of known espionage agents yielded no prints to match those he sought. Puzzled, Jimmy Christopher turned to still another case which contained the prints of all officers and enlisted men in the United States Army and Navy. Again his search was fruitless. Hesitating, he peered at a label designating a special sub-section of this file: *Deceased*. Obeying a strange impulse, he consulted it.

When he turned away, his eyes were dark, his lips hard-

TIM DONOVAN

pressed. Quietly he declared to the astounded Tim Donovan: "These are the prints of a dead man!"

"That's impossible, Jimmy!"

"But true, Tim! We know that modern science is able to resurrect the dead—we have seen the dead actually brought to life—but this is not such a case. The man who made these prints died, according to these reports, eighteen years ago!"

JIMMY CHRISTOPHER peered at the name on the card: *Major Rederick Bradshaw*. Beneath was a notation. *Died in airplane crash, Sissonne, France, May 25, 1917*. Quickly he restored the card, went to a special file, withdrew a photostatic copy of it, and tucked it into his pocket.

"We're dealing," he said so quietly that the Irish lad scarcely heard, "with a man strong enough to span the chasm of death—or with a madman!"

Again he examined the strange golden gun. Opening the cylinder, he saw that the slugs of each cartridge were indeed made of unalloyed gold, so soft that upon impact it would flatten and spatter, causing a ghastly wound. Grimly, he locked the weird weapon in a cabinet. He strode quickly from the Fingerprint Division to Z-7's office.

The Washington chief had just entered. His face was dour; his eyes were smouldering darkly. Operator 5 sensed Z-7's anxiety as he rapidly told his story of the night. He showed the photostat of the prints on the golden gun, and finished with:

"Made by a dead man—yet alive and aboard the *Monte Cristo* at this moment! Chief, don't I deserve to know why you ordered me off the case when we might have cracked it then and there?"

Z-7's blunt fingers drummed. "The army planes that went out from Mitchell Field on your alarm," he said gruffly, "managed to find the place you mentioned. But there was nothing suspicious about it. An estate closed up for the season. Certainly there were no planes or hangars in evidence. As for the leader of this espionage ring, as you term it, I have wirelessed the *Monte Cristo*.

The captain denies that he picked up any such passenger as you describe—that any such man is aboard."

Tim Donovan exclaimed, aghast: "But it's true, Chief! I was with Jimmy and saw the same thing!"

"You cannot question, Chief," Operator 5 insisted quietly, "that a devastating attack has been made upon us by some dangerous organization—!"

Z-7's eyes were piercing. "What the devil led you into this?" he demanded. "Why have you ignored orders to keep out of it? I don't intend to hold you for breaking away from me last night, when you were my prisoner, but I demand a full explanation."

"It's my practice, Chief, to be sure of myself before I turn in any information. I spotted men known to be international espionage agents—and I sought the thing they might be interested in. I found it—in the secret operations of the General Staff!"

"Whom have you spotted?" Z-7 demanded.

"A man named Wanvig, now dead—a dangerous saboteur. Another named Markoe; still another named Kurze. They are working together under the direction of the man in the golden mask—Major Rederick Bradshaw, dead these eighteen years—executing a master plan designed to crush the United States!"

AGAIN Z-7'S blunt fingers drummed, and Operator 5 went on: "There are always subversive activities within this country because we are the richest prize in the world—because we are wide open to secret attack. You know as well as I, Chief, that the foreign-financed, revolutionary organizations within the United States are stronger than the people suspect, a force to be seriously reckoned with."

"But this international espionage ring you speak of," Z-7 said quietly, "is not Communistic in nature."

"No. It is even more powerful. It is striking in a way we do not suspect. That man in the golden mask spoke of crushing us with a weapon of gold. Chief, I want to do everything possible to serve my country in this crisis—but the bitter fact is that our secret enemies know more of our operations than I do!"

"It is not unusual for governments to engage in strategies which even their political leaders know nothing about," Z-7 pointed out. "France is a very good example of that. As for the United States—" Z-7's fist thumped to the desk. "You have penetrated so far into this matter that now the whole of it must be disclosed to you. You shall share the secret."

Operator 5 smiled tightly. "I hope that I will be able to help," he said simply.

"The cargo of the *Rescuer*, which was completely destroyed by incendiary bombs last night, was—tin!"

Jimmy Christopher's eyes widened. "A strategic material, absolutely necessary to our defenses—a metal we cannot produce ourselves!"*

* AUTHOR'S NOTE: In his startling communication in The Secret Sentinel last month, the Chief disclosed the utter dependence of the United States on foreign supply for just one of the many materials vital to the waging of war—tin. The Chief's communication pointed out that tin is an absolute necessity to the manufacture of munitions, and that the United States produces virtually no tin. Great Britain, through the International Tin Committee controls more than ninety per cent of the world's supply

"Exactly!" the Washington chief exclaimed. "Tin is a vital necessity to us. In time of war, lack of tin might easily cripple us. The General Staff recently decided to lay in a secret store of tin. We have purchased large stocks of it; it was our intention to keep it hidden. Our secret leaked out somehow—and now all our careful preparations have failed."

"You bought this tin," Operator 5 asked, "from the British syndicate controlling the metal?"

"No. We were able to find a better price from a sub-syndicate. Our attempts to investigate it got nowhere. That did not matter, so long as we obtained the tin. Now there is a dangerous international organization working secretly against us. For, in order to buy the tin, we were obliged to sign contracts stipulating payment in gold on demand."

"A dangerous bargain, Chief!"

"We safeguarded ourselves with a gentleman's agreement that the gold would not be demanded during a period of five years. That agreement was promptly broken, and we had no redress. The ship you sighted last night—the *Monte Cristo*—was carrying one of the largest cargoes of gold bullion ever to leave our

of tin. The Chief pointed out that as far as the supply of the United States of vital tin is concerned, we are at the complete mercy of the International Tin Committee—British controlled. In other words, a single act of a single nation could, in time of war, stop all shipment of tin to the United States and cripple all our fighting units.

This is just one example of the complete dependence of the United States upon foreign sources of supply for many vital materials of warfare.

Treasury. That was why—because of the ticklish international situation—I ordered you off the investigation."

Z-7's fist slammed; and he jerked to his feet. "The damnable syndicate through which the United States has contracted for her stores of strategic materials—materials we must have but cannot produce sufficiently ourselves—tin, mercury, rubber, silk, wool, countless chemicals—has us jockeyed into such a position that we don't dare move. We must pay in gold. If we don't, our supply of vital strategic materials will be cut off. If we pay partially, then stop, the syndicate will broadcast the fact that our gold supply has become insufficient to support our monetary system.

"Yet, if we continue to pay, our Treasury will be drained. We must keep that fact secret, or it will mean panic. God! No matter which way we move, we face danger. That is why we have kept these operations so strictly secret."

OPERATOR 5 said quietly: "This plan, Chief, robs us of gold—the very basis of the nation's existence in this financial world—and gives us military materials which the undercover ring is operating to destroy as fast as we receive them!"

Z-7 peered, amazement and sudden understanding in his eyes.

"The man in the golden mask declared that tonight, at midnight, they will strike again. He promised for tomorrow night the destruction of the largest plant in the United States supplying us with ammunition and munitions against a national emergency. That can mean only the great Warwick Works in Delaware."

Z-7 gasped in dismay: "The destruction of that plant will cripple our rearmament program—ruin our plan to store munitions against future necessity!"

"It will, Chief!" Jimmy Christopher straightened. "This Service is now under the command of the Secretary of State. He should know of this at once. The Warwick Works must be guarded tonight as never before. We cannot tell how the ring will strike—therefore we must be prepared for any emergency. We are undermanned—we will need every agent available!"

"I'll inform the Secretary at once!" Z-7 took up the telephone. Operator 5, leaning over the desk intently, declared:

"We must consider above all else the General Staff's program. The United States has always been dependent on foreign sources for its supplies of war, and we absolutely must make ourselves self-sufficient. That is what the espionage ring is trying to keep us from doing—that is the goal we must achieve unless we wish to remain helpless before the world!"

Z-7 SPOKE crisply into the telephone. Jimmy Christopher noted the lines of his face grow deeper. His clipped monosyllables rang over the line; and a stubbornly fixed tone answered him. When he hung up his ebon eyes were smouldering, his mouth was a grim line.

"I have persuaded the Secretary to send men to the Warwick plant tonight, but he fixed the number at only twenty."

"Only twenty!" Operator 5 exclaimed. "Good Lord, Chief, the plant extends over a vast area. The attack might come from any angle. We should have a hundred men there—otherwise we can scarcely protect the plant at all!"

"Twenty, and no more, the Secretary has ordered," Z-7 answered flatly, "and I must obey his commands. He has given me special orders for you, Operator 5."

Operator 5 frowned apprehensively. "And those special orders, Chief?"

"Have to do with the secret organization known as the Hidden Hundred," Z-7 declared, gazing levelly into Jimmy Christopher's darkening eyes. "He knows that it will become powerless without the skill and shrewdness of its leader. He is concentrating on capturing that man!"

"He has given standing orders to every Intelligence operator to track down the leader of the Hidden Hundred—I know, Chief," Operator 5 murmured.

"Now," Z-7 went on, "he has charged you with capturing that man and unmasking him—of gathering sufficient evidence so that the sentence of death may be imposed upon him!"

Operator 5 stood white-faced. With grim quiet, Z-7 added: "You have never yet failed any orders given you, Operator 5. I trust on this detail you will be as successful."

Jimmy Christopher answered tersely: "I'll do my best, Chief!"

He strode from the office briskly, Tim Donovan at his side, anxiously studying his face. His eyes were dark with an ominous dread; his ears were ringing with the ominous words: "… the sentence of death… imposed upon him!"

CHAPTER 4
VOW OF THE SKELETONS

OVER A secret strand in the web of the Capital's telephone system, that night, impulses fluttered to ring a muted bell in a room which was utterly dark, which was concealed completely from the workaday world of Washington. The dim light which glowed inside it was only a spark dimly outlining the man who answered the summons. He did not speak when he lifted the receiver; but a whispered signal came over the line.

"Yes, captain!" he exclaimed alertly. "X-13 on duty!"

The hushed voice on the wire continued: "X-13, we already know that the man in the gold mask is putting a new plan of destruction into operation tonight. I believe I have learned where his blow will fall. The Secretary of State has not ordered the Intelligence to act on Operator 5's warning—therefore, the task is ours."

"Yes, captain!"

"Tonight," the whispering voice continued, "an entire train of vital freight is due in the capital. It is a shipment of mercury. I have learned that this is part of the General Staff's secret program. Their plan is to store the mercury immediately. The man in the gold mask must certainly intend to disrupt these plans. We must do everything possible to insure the safety of the shipment. X-13—orders!"

"Yes, captain!"

The man in the black room listened intently to the commanding words which came over the wire. When he cradled the receiver, a plan was formed—a plan to be transmitted to, and acted upon, by a band of secret guardians of the nation's safety. Under the cover of darkness, the strategy became translated into undercover action.

Darkness lay over the intricate maze of gleaming tracks of the freight yards of the nation's capital. Over this puzzle of steel lines, locomotive headlights gleamed, pistons snorted, yard engines chuffed back and forth. Thousands of boxcars, some empty and some awaiting the unloading crews, stood on the tracks. Into the deep shadows surrounding them there came strange, furtive presences.

They appeared out of nowhere, following secret orders—men who were seemingly phantoms. They moved and spoke, yet in the gloom, their heads appeared fleshless skulls; their hands, the bony claws of skeletons. Unseen by the yard crews and the watchmen, they had materialized out of the night; their meeting places, the deepest gloom. From the sockets of their skulls, bright, alert eyes gleamed, watching the operations of the yards.

At a score of strategic points throughout the great yards these ghostly figures lurked. They were the dread, fearless organization which the Intelligence had been ordered to stamp out of existence. It was the leader of this courageous band whom Operator 5 had been ordered to capture. These strange beings with the skull heads and the skeleton hands were the Hidden Hundred....

A group of these spectral figures, huddled in deep gloom at the side of the yards, was startled by a commanding presence who appeared among them. They looked upon the masked eyes of the man who was their secret leader, and heard him speak softly:

"The freight train is now entering the yards. Every car of it is loaded with mercury. It is guarded by a number of army officers not in uniform. It is going to be backed onto a siding, but it will not be unloaded for several hours. General Staff will then send army trucks to unload it, and before that, troops will take charge of these yards, and every hiding place will be searched."

The captain of the Hidden Hundred surveyed the spreading fans of tracks as he spoke.

"You hear the engine of the freight now—it's coming near. Chief of Staff's arrangement means that the man in the gold mask must strike before the troops take charge of the yards. It means that we must be prepared for an immediate attack, that we must complete our work before the troops arrive. Otherwise we will be outnumbered, cornered, our organization destroyed. You already have your orders. Hold yourself ready."

"Yes, captain!"

THE LEADER of the Hidden Hundred vanished. He passed to another group, to repeat his information to them. Each moment brought nearer the cunning move on the part of the gold-masked man's organization. The fate of a costly shipment of vital military material hung in the balance as the minutes passed.

The slow-moving freight was crawling into the great yards. Its engine snorted and labored as it tugged the string of cars toward the siding on which it was to wait. From the cabin of the locomotive, the engineer peered ahead, watching the beam of the headlight. Beside him stood a man in smart civilian suit; his bearing was erect, his movements brisk; he was a man of military training. Lieutenant George Judson was one of the plainclothes crew guarding the vital shipment.

Judson turned back, climbed to the top of the first boxcar, surveyed the gloomy yards. Other army officers in plainclothes were stationed at intervals along the line of cars. Still others were in the caboose. All of them were alert and armed. They searched the darkness—seeing no suggestion of an attack, unaware that the Hidden Hundred were hovering near—while the trucks of the cars clattered over a switch.

In a moment, these men believed, their trying trip would be at an end. They did not suspect that it would end, for most of them, with—death!

A sharp report echoed through the snorting of the engine. The snapping burst startled Judson. Peering, he leveled his automatic. Still he saw nothing strange around him; he knew only that the train was stopping. As it crashed to a standstill, each coupling thundering, air sneezing through the brake-hoses, he turned back to the locomotive. Bending to climb down, he stopped short.

The engineer was no longer at the throttle. The man in grimy coveralls was lying on the steel floor, face up, eyes staring, blood coloring the side of his face. It had poured from a ghastly bullet wound in the side of his head. Chilled, Judson peered at the fallen engineer.

A bullet had killed him—a bullet fired from somewhere in

the gloom of the yards—and Judson had heard the report. Now, out of the darkness, came the sound of quick movements. Men were running through the shadows. In the gleam of the headlight, Judson caught fast glimpses of these strange figures. They were clothed skeletons, running, guns gripped in bony fingers.

A shout of alarm rose to Judson's lips—but it was stifled by a cry that echoed from one of his brother-officers stationed near the end of the train. It was a shout of consternation and terror. "Move the train! The engine's heading right into us! It's going to crash!"

The blinding gleam of a headlight played along the side of the freight as an engine came chuffing along a track that angled into the switch. The freight had come to a stop before it had passed this intersection of tracks. The switch lay below the string of mercury-freighted boxcars. The approaching engine, roaring like an angry dragon, was bearing directly toward the center of the line of cars loaded with vital war material!

FRANTIC SHOUTS blended into the driving noises of the pistons as the plainclothes guardians of the strategic cargo called their warning. It had no effect on the roaring locomotive which was bearing down on them. That engine did not slow. The man in coveralls, who was peering out of the cab, must see the cars directly ahead of him in the shine of the headlight— he must know that a collision was imminent—yet he did not slow his locomotive. It plunged upon the string of mercury cars like a juggernaut. Only seconds could pass before the inevitable crash....

Judson whirled frantically. He leaped into the locomotive

cab where the engineer lay dead with a bullet through the brain. His one thought was to open the throttle to its limit, to pull the freight cars forward and away from the thundering danger. Yet even as he made the move, he knew it was hopeless. He could not possibly get the freight underway in time. The charging engine must inexorably plunge into it....

Judson reached for the throttle—and again the spiteful whine of a bullet sounded through the bedlam. Judson staggered back, blinded by blood. He fired once, wildly, and his bullet whistled harmlessly into the darkness. He grabbed again at the throttle and missed. Stiffly, he plunged forward. His body rolled once and lay limp beside the engineer. The roar of the onrushing engine was lost forever to his ears.

Straight to the center of the string of cars loaded with mercury the snarling engine plunged. As the distance melted to yards, the engineer whirled from his throttle. He leaped from one side of the cab while another coveralled man sprang from the other. They abandoned the engine while it was speeding with crushing momentum. They sprawled in the grit, jerked up, poised to run.

They found themselves surrounded by glinting guns—by automatics leveled in skeleton hands. "Hold them prisoner!" a commanding voice shouted. "Engines—both ends! Take it—"

A deafening crash broke into the words. The driving power of the manless engine struck the side of the string of motionless cars. The tremendous impact drove it through splintering wood which a moment before had been a loaded freight. The terrific shock derailed the juggernaut when it had driven completely through. It crunched to a stop on the farther side of the mercury string, pulling a single flatcar behind it.

That car came to a stop among the debris—and destruction flared from it. Blinding white fire sent a glare over the entire yards. Withering heat played into the wreckage of the broken car, and flames spread swiftly. The flaring light played over crates plunging from the broken cars that tumbled to their sides. Out of the wreckage poured silver liquid—precious mercury, trickling from cracked flasks. Streams and pools of glistening silver flickered in the glare of rising flames as havoc struck along the length of the freight.

Ringing orders carried through the increasing roar. In the red gleam, ghostly figures raced, following desperate instructions. While flames played along the freight—flames spread by the terrific heat of sizzling thermite—skull-headed men leaped into the locomotive where two men lay dead. Their guns flashed in their hands as they took charge. An opened throttle spun the drivers of the engine and its power passed through clashing couplings.

SLOWLY THE engine began to move, its force liberated by a skeleton band. It began to pull after it those cars which were still on the rails, though blazing. Along the string, daring the destructive heat, other masked men raced, loosening couplings. Derailed cars were detached—and a panting engine began to pull a parade of flame behind it, away from the blistering destruction of corrosive thermite.

The shrill scream of a fire-siren carried over the yards while other squads of the Hidden Hundred raced into action. While other couplings were opened, an engine came panting along the same track, toward the end of the string. Masked men had sped to it, following the ringing commands of their leader. At the point of guns, they had driven the yard crew from it. Now in command, they sped the switch engine to the caboose of the mercury freight.

Ghostly beings in the frightening flare of fire, they coupled the end of the freight to their engine. Immediately its drivers spun on the rails in reverse. Its mammoth power tugged at the blazing rear cars. It began drawing a part of the precious shipment of freight away from the center of the chaotic conflagration. At both ends of the string, engines were chugging under full power, pulling the two sections apart.

Tracks were melting under the terrific heat of the spreading thermite when more men of the Hidden Hundred charged into the blinding white light. They sprang into deadly heat as another locomotive approached. It came chuffing along the track that had carried the juggernaut of destruction. Faint and breathless in the withering heat, they dashed across red-hot tracks, giving frantic assistance to the crew in the cab of the approaching engine. Their clothing burst out in flame as they sped back.

Another coupling crashed; drivers spun again; and the third engine began to draw backward, carrying with it the car from which thermite was still spewing. It was a wheeled thing that disintegrated even as it rolled. Its path was marked by streaming, molten iron. Blinded, staggered by the murderous heat, the masked men in the cab kept backing until the juggernaut crunched off the rails.

Now the force of destruction was moved from the spot where two freight cars lay wrecked and blazing among others that were toppled over and derailed. The white flames streaked up in an open area, and from this spot no fire could spread. The sneezing and snorting of locomotives continued while the two other engines continued to pull the sections of the freight apart. With them went cars loaded with mercury, their sides flaming, but their cargo as yet unharmed.

The screaming of the fire-siren brought a frantic yard crew rushing. The shrill note was echoed from far parts of the capital as the alarm spread and city fire-fighting units began a race to the spot. In the mad confusion and the blinding glare, men in skull masks were everywhere. In the terrific first crash, several army officers had perished; those who escaped rushed appalled from the scene, too stunned to attempt to capture those of the Hidden Hundred who sped past.

Across the great freight yards, men in plainclothes dashed. As the Hidden Hundred scattered, they recognized these men who ran with guns in their hands, with their eyes grim and hard. They were regular operators of the Intelligence, dispatched in fast cars to the yards at the first alarm that the Hidden Hundred was operating. The undercover agents acting under the orders of Z-7 scattered through the maze of tracks—but in the confusing roar of the fire, they caught no glimpse of any of the living skeletons. THEY FOUND two broken strings of freights containing vital military material—now safe. They discovered that the worst threat of the attack had been counteracted by the swift strategy of the skull-masked men. They discovered, lying bound and

helpless, four men in coveralls whom they recognized immediately as dangerous international espionage agents. But of the
Hidden Hundred they found not a sign…!

The report of the leader of the Intelligence detail came by
telephone into WDC-13: "Z-7! B-8 reporting! The fire in the
yards is under control; no more damage will be done. Four cars
and their freight have been lost—but only four! All the rest are
saved—due, thank God, to the action of the Hidden Hundred!
Its members escaped after saving the freight, but they left prisoners for us. We have four men who engineered this attack—all
dangerous saboteurs—we have them prisoners, thanks again to
the Hidden Hundred!"

Z-7's crackling retort was: "The leader of that secret band—
was he there? Did he escape?"

"He was here—he must have been! He got away clean, Chief!
Whether we like to admit it or not, we are much obliged to him
for the fact that the entire string of cars wasn't destroyed!"

Grimly Z-7 answered: "Search those yards! Try to find that
man! You have standing orders to capture the leader of the
Hidden Hundred!"

Fire still blazed high in the great yards—fire which erased
the shadows in which the Hidden Hundred had lurked. The
darkness was gone; and with it, the secret band and its cunning
leader had vanished…!

THE ROOM was black and soundless. It might have been
an empty room; yet there were strange presences. Here loyal
soldiers of secrecy, sworn to preserve the safety of their nation,
were meeting in guarded conclave.

These men of mystery stood waiting while, again and again, the dark drapes of the walls parted and others entered to stand as silently as they. An undercover summons had brought them. A common purpose bound them—service to a government which had renounced them! They were just as courageously devoted to the cause of the welfare of the United States as the President and the General Staff, yet they were hunted men. They were the Hidden Hundred!

A soft rustle sounded in the gloom as the black drapes parted again. Those waiting sensed a commanding presence. Before them, a dim shine appeared. The glow brightened to fill the entire room, disclosing the strange masks worn by each member of the Hidden Hundred. Their heads appeared to be fleshless skulls, with bright, alert eyes shining from bony sockets. Their hands seemed to be skeleton claws. They faced now, in that secret room, the man who was their captain.

He stood behind a black table, wearing white-marked hood and gloves—seemingly a clothed skeleton like his comrades. His eyes shone dark blue as he surveyed their ghastly faces. His voice sounded muffled through his mask as he addressed them:

"Comrades. Tonight, due to your swift action—your readiness to risk death in the service of your country—we destroyed one of the plans of the man in the golden mask. Though he remains as securely hidden as before, we have crippled his organization by capturing four members of it; we fought him and won! I greet you in the brotherhood of a common cause—and pay you homage!"

The room was silent.

"We are confronted by dangerous risks—not only from the powerful forces at work against the United States, but from our friends of the Intelligence Service. We know the penalty we face is death—yet we cannot hesitate to take up the challenge. I bring you orders."

THE MEN with the skull heads gazed with admiring fascination at their leader. All of them had once been loyal operators in the United States Intelligence. Their low pay and endless hours had not kept them from giving a full measure of devotion to the Service. Yet, without warning, an ultimatum from the Secretary of State had dismissed them.

It was this masked man, facing them now, who had drawn them together into the powerful, secret organization of the Hidden Hundred. Realizing that the Service was hamstrung by the Secretary's edict, they had pledged themselves to keep it strong even though they themselves were excluded from it. They were ready now, when their former comrades in the Service hunted them feverishly, to obey the commands of their unknown leader.

He spoke quietly: "Our nation is striving to erect a permanent peace; yet we must be prepared against war. We have already established means of maintaining our neutrality in case of a new world conflict,* yet we must arm ourselves against the danger of being drawn into it. Destructive forces are at work against

---

* AUTHOR'S NOTE: The State Department has a comprehensive program to safeguard United States neutrality in the event of war abroad. This plan would prevent American citizens from sailing on ships registered by bellig-

us—forces too powerful for our crippled Intelligence to cope with—and danger lies on every hand. Upon the work of the Hidden Hundred largely rests the preservation of the nation. We face a secret battle against a foe we cannot see."

The clothed skeletons listened intently.

"You appreciate as deeply as I the many subversive forces within the United States. Of these, Communism is only one—and it is a force far weaker than the power we confront today. Let it suffice now, because every moment is precious, to say that our task is to do everything possible to prevent the utter destruction of the great Warwick Works tonight!"

A murmur of appalled astonishment passed among the men in the skull masks.

"Comrade X-13 carries your written orders. You will destroy them upon reading them. Before you act, you will await my signal. We will undertake them only if the Intelligence itself is rendered helpless to cope with the situation.

"If the signal is given, you may be captured by men who are your friends—members of the Intelligence. You all know what

erents. Without such a prohibition the death of one or two citizens aboard a torpedoed foreign liner might involve the country in war.

Another feature would bar permanently from United States citizenship any citizen who enlisted in a foreign military or naval force. The shipment from the United States of cargoes of any kind aboard belligerent ships. Armed merchantmen would be barred from United States ports. The use of United States ports as coaling stations for belligerent nations would be prohibited.

that means. Yet we must do our utmost to prevent the enemy's destructive blow.

"Take orders!"

The light behind the captain of the Hidden Hundred faded and went out. The rustle of draperies again sounded. The men in the skull masks passed silently into an adjoining room. There they received their orders from the member designated X-13. When the final black envelope was passed among them, X-13 bade them wait the signal. He stepped through black curtains and went quietly to a rear room—the headquarters of the commander of the Hidden Hundred.

He found it empty. On the black desk lay a single square of scrawled paper. The claw hand of X-13 raised it, and the eyes glittered in their bony sockets as the man read the dread message:

> Urgent orders for your capture have been issued to Operator 5.
>
> X-55.

The captain of the Hidden Hundred had already departed on a mission that promised death!

OPERATOR 5 strode briskly into a secluded office of the State, War and Navy Building in Washington. He paused, confronting the hard-faced, cold-eyed Secretary of State. He saw frank hostility in the Secretary's eyes, as he said:

"Sir, I have come to plead with you to detail more Intelligence men to protection of the Warwick Works tonight."

"I'm to order the whole Intelligence to concentrate—to satisfy your unfounded suspicions?" the Secretary snapped.

"We cannot ignore the power operating against us, sir. The whole Intelligence is scarcely strong enough now for the task facing us tonight."

The Secretary leaned forward sternly. "I have Z-7's report on your information. In it, the name of Haigh is mentioned—the Ambassador from the Court of St. James! That seems to indicate that the plot to drain our Treasury is of British origin. And obviously that is untrue."

"Obviously!" Jimmy Christopher nodded. "But Haigh's name is being used by the lieutenant of the man in the gold mask as a cover. The fact that the *Monte Cristo* is a British ship is a deliberate trick to arouse our suspicions. Most of all, we might suspect Great Britain because of the present economic war between her and this country. This only proves how deeply hidden the real power is—how cunningly it is moving against us."

The Secretary challenged: "Well?"

"We need all our manpower to combat it. The Intelligence should be enlarged to its old scope, sir; the men discharged by your order a month ago should be reinstated. Only in that way can we—"

"Reinstate them?" the Secretary snapped. "They are now members of the Hidden Hundred! They are discredited, subversive, illegal workers. That treasonable organization shall be stamped out. Your orders, Operator 5, are to get its leader!"

"Yes, sir," Operator 5 said tightly. "But I must point out to you, sir, that failure to strengthen the Intelligence encourages the Hidden Hundred to continue its work—because it must!"

The Secretary's eyes narrowed. "I await the report of your attempt to capture the leader of the Hidden Hundred, Operator 5," he said levelly, "with the keenest interest."

Operator 5 turned briskly. When he paused at the door his lips curled wryly. "If this plan succeeds it means panic—financial destruction of the richest country in the world." His tone grew bitter. "We are building the strongest treasure house in the world for our gold—and yet we are letting a secret enemy drain it!"

He closed the door smartly, strode away. Walking swiftly along Pennsylvania Avenue until he reached a busy commercial corner, he entered a store and slipped into a telephone booth. His eyes were grave, darkened with deep concern, as he called a secret number.

Far across the city a muffled bell rang in a black-walled room. The skeleton hand of X-13 raised it. Over the line, Operator 5 said crisply:

"Follow orders!"

The captain of the Hidden Hundred had given his signal to act!

OVER A dark road on the outskirts of a great city in Delaware, a parade of swift cars sped. Gleaming headlamps probed deep into the night. Those autos carried grim-faced men bent upon following a secret command. They were soldiers of secrecy, selected as the ablest of the Hidden Hundred. Their destination was the world-famous Warwick Munition Works.

Jimmy Christopher wrapped his hands tightly on the wheel

of the sleek roadster which led the way. From Washington this detail of his men had been transported secretly to this center of tonight's strategy. Ahead, in open country, its position marked by the flames shooting skyward from its gigantic chimneys, lay the nation's greatest ammunition factory and steel mill.

The music issuing softly from the radio of Operator 5's roadster ceased exactly at eleven-thirty. An announcer introduced a program of news comments. The first item brought an alert gleam into Jimmy Christopher's eyes.

"Since Great Britain and Japan abandoned the gold standard, followed by the United States, widespread anxiety has increased as to the position of France, Switzerland and other nations in world finance. A general abandonment of the gold standard will mean world chaos, and the struggle of the United States to maintain her relative position will mean inflation on a wild scale—the same chaos which swamped Germany at the end of the World War."

Operator 5 well knew the dangerous example cited. Rapid printing of paper money by Germany, backed by a dwindling, and at last negligible, treasury, once begun, had gained uncontrollable momentum. As the value of marks decreased, huge sums were necessary to buy the ordinary necessities of life. A loaf of bread cost a hundred thousand marks in the morning, hundreds of thousands more by night. The moment came when a million mark note was useful only to light fires. Jimmy Christopher's heart grew cold at the thought of the same financial madness devaluating the dollar and spreading monetary havoc in the United States.

"Criticism of the President's recovery program is increasing," the broadcast continued. "The gigantic sums spent on public works and on relief are, the President's political opponents believe, undermining the stability of the nation. The eyes of the world are on us—and fear is growing of a worldwide financial collapse if the United States' system should show any indication of crumbling."

Jimmy Christopher clicked the radio off and whispered: "Gold—a weapon of destruction even more powerful than the munitions being manufactured in the Warwick Works tonight!" IN THE sky, the flare of flames from the converters and chimneys of the great mills grew brighter. Nearing the great plant, Jimmy Christopher turned into a side-road. The cars carrying the members of the Hidden Hundred followed as he swerved again into a field. Deep into the shadows, their headlamps clicked off now, they crawled; at last, in the thickest darkness, they stopped.

Out of the cars the men came. They paused, fixing on their heads the grotesque masks, pulling the skeletal gloves on their hands. Like phantoms, they gathered around Operator 5's roadster, standing off at a distance and awaiting his signal. At Jimmy Christopher's side stood the man who had distributed his orders for action—the man designated X-13.

His name was John Christopher, and once his designation had been Operator Q-6 in the United States Intelligence. A serious wound had forced him to retire from the Service. Two bullets lay so close to his heart that no surgeon dared try to remove them. They threatened him constantly with death. Yet, he dedicated himself now to the service of the Hidden Hundred under the leadership of his son.

His attempt to rejoin the Intelligence had been balked by the curt refusal on the part of the Secretary of State; he had chosen to shoulder the risk of working at Operator 5's side; and his designation was that of a man who had died.

Quietly Jimmy Christopher said: "It's impossible to guess from which direction the blow will fall, Dad. We know only that the man in the gold mask has undoubtedly planned with the utmost shrewdness. The attack may come from the river, from the air, across the ground—no one can tell."

"You've done your best with the plans," ex-Operator Q-6 answered, "and you can count on us to the limit!"

Operator 5 signaled his men closer. They followed him to a stone wall, crossed it. Beyond, in a vast open area, the great Warwick Works sprawled. A high mesh fence completely enclosed the rambling, sooty buildings. Inside it, armed guards of the plant police were patrolling; added to their numbers tonight were the twenty Intelligence men detailed by the Secretary of State.

One of the skull-masked men touched Operator 5. He was X-27, known to Jimmy Christopher as one of the ablest operators ever to work with the Intelligence—one of the most courageous men of the secret band. He said with quiet urgency:

"There is no need for you to endanger yourself, Captain. Leave the job entirely to us. You're in greater danger than any of us, in case of capture. We have nothing to lose, but you—"

Jimmy Christopher's eyes twinkled. "I won't ask any of you," he declared quietly, "to do anything I would hesitate to do myself. I'm more than willing to run the risk.... We're ready!"

His men moved forward with him with the certainty of careful planning. They became scattering, black shadows in the open around the high fence. Noiselessly they took positions near it, while Operator 5 led the way toward one of the great gates. Across the black ground he peered, while an armed sentry patrolled past. Once the guard was marching beyond, he darted to the gate.

Each move he made, each move of the men with him, was a timed maneuver. He gripped a huge pair of cutters handed him by one masked man. He closed the powerful, sharp blades on the chain which fastened the gate. The links parted at once. He slipped his automatic into his hand, opened the way, darted through. While his men remained outside, he backed—melting into the flickering gloom.

The sentry was returning. When he was directly opposite the gate, Operator 5 stepped forward. The grinding of his heel in the grit jerked a startled response from the guard. The sooty-faced man whirled to see an apparition approaching him—a being with a skull for a head, with claws for hands—a skeleton garbed like a living man. He lifted his rifle, stunned with astonishment, but the butt never reached his shoulder.

OPERATOR 5'S stiffened fingers drove to his neck. A deft twist exerted paralyzing force upon a vital nerve center. The effect of the lightning ju-jitsu blow was to freeze the man with the rifle. He drew in a sharp breath, tottered rigidly, began to fall.

Operator 5 caught him, lowered him, and through the fabric of his mask murmured: "Sorry, old man!"

Instantly, the skull-masked men rushed in through the gate. Two of them lifted the unconscious guard, carried him into deeper shadows near the building wall. Others scattered toward posts assigned them in their secret orders. Operator 5 waited tensely, X-13 at his side, while the vague figures vanished in the flickering gloom.

Presently a man in grimy overalls, carrying a rifle, his face greasy with soot, reappeared at the gate and began patrolling slowly back and forth. He was not one of the company guards. He was X-66, member of the Hidden Hundred.

Now Operator 5 stood alone against a black doorway, peering all around. The passing minutes were bringing the zero hour— the moment of the planned attack—closer. Quietly, efficiently, the members of the Hidden Hundred were making ready to parry the blow when it fell, while facing a double danger themselves.

Into the great plant, at intervals, overalled men sauntered from the yards. The passes they showed the armed watchmen enabled them to move beyond the guarded doors, into the vast reaches of the humming works. They, too, were members of the Hidden Hundred acting upon secret orders.

Within these walls, munitions and ammunition were being made upon order of the United States government, to be stored against a future national emergency. Giant converters were pouring into flaming ladles molten steel which was soon to become cannon. In another plant, within fireproof walls, guarded with

the utmost care, men and women were laboring at the dangerous task of making projectiles of all sizes. Night and day, the
entire works was functioning to provide the government with
the strength which, until now, it had sadly lacked.

At one of the gates, a car stopped. From it, a girl alighted. She
was in her early twenties, very pretty, her manner one of confidence. To the sentries at the gate she displayed a pass. It bore
the name *Ruth Wilson*, the designation *telephone switchboard
operator* and the notation hours *12 to 6 a.m.* Examining it, the
guard asked: "You're new, ain't you?"

"My first night here," the girl answered.

"Go ahead."

She smiled faintly as she drove into the sooty yard—glad
that the forged pass had deceived the guard. It was in truth her
first night at the plant, but it was to be her only one. Her name
was really Diane Elliot. She was not a switchboard operator at
all, but a special reporter for the far-flung Amalgamated Press.
More important, she was a courageous friend whom Operator
5 trusted implicitly, who had aided him tremendously in previous difficult cases. She, too, was following the secret orders of
the leader of the Hidden Hundred.

She entered the huge executive building of the Warwick
Works, went to the room in which the telephone system of the
plant centered. At one of the long banks of switchboards, she
took up her duties. Peering around intently, she saw on one wall
a glass-covered case in which open knife-switches glittered.

These, Operator 5 had told her, were connected to the
alarm-gongs scattered throughout the great works. Closing the

switches would flash a danger signal everywhere in the rambling buildings. Diane Elliot's attention fixed on those electric blades as she automatically made routine calls at her board.

HIDDEN BY the darkness of the open, Operator 5 watched anxiously. The zero hour was nearly at hand. He peered upward into the black zenith; he strained his ears to listen. The previous attack had come by air. If the same medium were used in the attack tonight, the agents of destruction would find the night sky well policed by the Hidden Hundred.

Far above, unseen and unheard, autogyros were hovering. They floated high beyond the flare of the chimney fires. In one, a man designated X-43, was at the controls, and a boy, leaning over the cowling, was searching the dark ground through powerful binoculars. Tim Donovan kept alert for any signal that might flash upward to him. Close at hand, he kept a Very pistol, ready to relay that signal, when it came, to other gyros flitting in the night sky. In those other pits, pilots of the Hidden Hundred carried high-explosive bombs.

Over a wide area, Operator 5's men were waiting tensely.

A black river flowed past the gritty territory occupied by the Warwick Works. It was patrolled as carefully as the walls; but now agents of the Hidden Hundred were also stationed there secretly. Huge locked gates barred the piers: the water flowed like ink below. All around the works, the night lay thick; and from the buildings issued a continual rumbling.

The Hidden Hundred were ready!

Operator 5's nerves tightened and he shrank back in his hiding place. Heels were gritting on the ground; men were

HOSTS OF THE FLAMING DEATH

Thermite projectiles
screamed from the deck-guns
of the submarine to destroy
the vast munitions plant!

approaching. They came nearer, and in the shine of the chimney fires, Jimmy Christopher glimpsed faces he knew. These were operators of the United States Intelligence. They were part of the hopelessly small detail sent by the Secretary of State—a greater danger to the Hidden Hundred than to the unseen, lurking attackers.

The Intelligence men moved quickly through the shadows, melted from sight. Their orders were also placing them at strategic points. Under cover of the night, they stationed themselves near the outlaw soldiers of secrecy whom they had been ordered to capture!

Still, through the slits of his mask, Jimmy Christopher peered around. He had arranged a system of signaling by which a warning of danger might be flashed from any point within the works. A glance at his watch told him that it was midnight. His nerves grew hot with anxiety while the final seconds ticked away.

Zero hour!

At one of the gates which opened onto the loading piers—great, flat structures which fingered out into the black river—a man in coveralls paused. He was X-89 of the Hidden Hundred. Hearing a curious lapping sound, he peered at the rippling blackness. Startled, dismayed, he glimpsed vague, gray outlines appearing in the water. A moment ago, the river had been empty. Now a strange craft was visible—a thing that had risen from the black depths. A submarine!

X-89 whirled, whipped a pocket torch from his pocket and touched its contact. The lens was taped so that only a pencil beam appeared—a spark which flickered in code signal. It twinkled across the gritty ground to Operator 5. Its quick message was: *Attack by river!*

Instantly, Jimmy Christopher turned his own torch skyward. All the plans he had formed were immediately discarded for one that became vital—a maneuver to repulse an attack coming over the water. His upturned light blinked a tiny spot skyward. Its beam flashed high—and it was caught by alert Tim Donovan. THE BOY, while his autogyro hovered against the ceiling, instantly loaded the Very pistol. Breathlessly, he pointed it, pulled the trigger. A red flare streaked through the high darkness, relaying the warning to four other gyros fluttering unseen around him. The color flashed: *Attack by river!* Instantly, the sky shook with the swift maneuvering of the vaned craft.

Operator 5, in his anxiety, moved out of the sheltering shadow, running forward in the hope of learning the full extent of the danger. His signals were not complete. Additional information must be flashed before the counterattack could strike at its mark. Seeking this vital information, he ran across the open space toward the river bank, peering at the sinister outlines etched against the rippling blackness of the water. From the shadows of the walls a shrill, prolonged whistle rang. Operator 5 heard it, knew it was no part of his prearranged plan—knew that it signaled danger to his Hidden Hundred—but the threat on the water forced him to ignore it. He raced forward....

He saw the submarine riding the black water. He realized, in a flash, that it had crept in from the open sea. Its hatches had opened; black-uniformed men were crowding upon its dripping superstructure. An officer was snapping commands and a gun crew was going into action. The barrel of the small cannon was raised toward the buildings of the Warwick Works; and even as he paused breathless near the mesh fence he heard the curt, distant command: "Fire!"

A booming burst of power broke from the muzzle of the gun. Out of a flare of flame a projectile streaked, its short trajectory marked by flying sparks. It curved down to the roof of the steel mills, and a dull concussion echoed as it struck. The darkness was torn by a flare of blinding white fire; and hissing stuff flew far over the spreading roofs.

Thermite projectiles! Corrosive destruction catapulted out of the deck gun of the submarine, calculated to destroy the machinery which was making munitions for the United States! Flaming havoc leaping out of the black waters of the river!

Operator 5 raised his light to flash an added signal—a blinking message which would inform the hovering gyros of the exact location of the sub—when swift footfalls sounded around him. Another shrill blast of a whistle rattled in his ears.

The desperate urgency of flashing the warning allowed him no time to notice the danger closing in around him. He pressed the contact button—and the torch was knocked from his hands.

He whirled to find grim-faced men circled around him, their automatics leveled. Intelligence operators! Brothers of Operator 5's undercover service—making the captain of the Hidden Hundred their captive!

CHAPTER 5
"NAME YOUR LEADER!"

"**S**TAND WHERE you are!" a sharp voice commanded Jimmy Christopher. "You're our prisoner."

Through the slits of his weird skull mask, Operator 5's eyes shone, pinched with dismay. Hands gripped his arms. One of the Intelligence men stepped forward to snatch his automatic away. Another growled, "Unmask him here and now!" But a second dull concussion shocked through the night, and a new flare of blinding, white light spewed over the buildings.

The submarine had blasted a second charge of thermite from its gun, into the very center of the giant plant!

Confusion stormed! Operator 5's words rang out: "Let me flash this signal! There are planes above ready to drop bombs on that sub! For God's sake, let me!"

The strong hands on Operator 5's arms tugged him away through the mad bedlam. A moan of dismay broke from his masked lips as he twisted to peer back. On the superstructure of the submarine, the gun crew was ramming another bursting charge of thermite into the breech. In a moment, a third destructive blow would be struck at the vital armament program of the United States. He strove to break away, to snatch the torch from the hand of the man who held it, to signal the warning into the sky—and a sob of futility came from his aching throat.

On the roof of the buildings, the sizzling thermite spread in white, corrosive pools. Swiftly, the intense heat ate through, dropped. Within the caverns below, it spilled upon gigantic machinery, radiating blinding light. Its destructive effect quickly ruined precious implements necessary to working steel. It unleashed molten metal that flowed like lava across the grit floor, and howls of terror broke from the workers who scattered in panic.

Down through another roof, the all-destroying stuff dropped. It fell around hoppers of explosive materials which were being used to fill explosive shells. A terrific concussion shook the walls as the stuff detonated, spreading havoc. Men and women stampeded frantically over the dead bodies of comrades who had worked at their sides a moment ago. Shrieks of terror rang more shrilly than the clanging of the alarm gongs throughout the corridors of the great works.

At the first blow, a member of the Hidden Hundred, stationed at a plant telephone, had flashed the warning to Diane Elliot at the switchboard. She had dashed to the glass-faced cabinet and shattered the pane with a single blow of the hammer hanging ready beside it. Her quick thrusts closed the contacts, one after another. Throughout the giant plant, gongs were signaling the fall of destruction. Now the girl swiftly plugged connections to summon all possible aid to the scene.

Through the scores of doors of the gigantic plant, men ran terrified to escape the buildings encompassed by the blinding white havoc. The stampeding thousands bore down the strong mesh fence; they ran in a frenzy into the roads. Among them, completely surrounded by Intelligence agents, went the man whose attempt to save the giant works from destruction had been balked—the leader of the Hidden Hundred!

Yet, high in the sky, the alertness of Tim Donovan was a hope of salvation. The light of the rising flames had disclosed to him the mysterious craft riding the black water of the river. Again he had loaded his Very pistol and flashed its red signal twice through the night. It ordered: "Follow me!" and brought the vaned craft swirling lower as his pilot streaked downward to the mark.

Out of the flaring sky, projectiles dropped. They whistled shrilly toward the underwater craft. A terrific explosion parted the water near its glistening hulk, sent black-uniformed men plunging from the superstructure. Immediately the rending concussion was followed by others as the gyros of the Hidden Hundred sent their explosive charges plummeting.

At the bank of the river, Intelligence men retreated from the force of the blasts. Withering submachine-gun fire from the superstructure whipped a number of them down, dead; sent others scurrying frantically for cover. Overpowered, dazed by the terrific counterattack from the sky, they ran for their lives while the Hidden Hundred darted from their stations.

Swiftly, from man to man of the outlaw undercover agents, a message passed. The roaring of the fire, the howling of the maddened crowd, the panic that spread around the flaming buildings, did not stop its swift course. It was an alarm which sent them fighting their way through the fleeing mob: "The Captain has been taken prisoner!"

A PRISONER—HELD at gunpoint by his comrades of the Intelligence Service! Operator 5, the weird mask still completely covering his face, had been forced off the grounds of the great works. Hands gripping his arms thrust him toward a car around which men, shouting in terror, were running. Near its side he was jerked to a stop. The operator in charge of the detail declared grimly:

"Now there's a chance to look at your face now! Remove your mask!"

A hand snatched at the drawstrings which held the skull-mask tight beneath the chin of Operator 5. It jerked them loose—and Jimmy Christopher's heart froze. Again the words of Z-7 echoed through his mind: "Execute the penalty of death upon him!" Despair such as he had never felt before gripped him as the fabric of the mask went loose upon his face—as the operator behind him began to lift it off.

Gunfire!

The blaze shot out of the night behind the ring of Intelligence agents. In consternation they whirled—and in the glare of the fire they glimpsed weird figures springing toward them. Some were garbed in overalls; some were wearing ordinary business suits; but all of them appeared to be fleshless skeletons. In their claw-hands, they gripped automatics that blazed defiance to the men who had once fought secret battles at their sides.

Operator 5 leaped back as the members of the Hidden Hundred attacked. Bullets sang overhead during the swift, desperate battle. He whirled into the car, ducked out the far side, struck hard into the face of the agent who crowded after him. The man dropped as Jimmy Christopher whirled across the road, shouldering and elbowing his way through the scattering mob of steelworkers. Out of the confusion, he heard the ringing voice of one of his lieutenants: "Keep 'em away from the Captain!"

Again guns blasted. Within the walls of the great ammunition plant, a series of rending explosions rocked. Along the roads, thousands scattered in terror. The blackness of the river surface had become churning turmoil from the plummeting of the bombs dropped by the hovering gyros. A muffled thunder of defiance came from the motors of the swooping craft commanded by Tim Donovan. He peered down at the submarine and saw water pouring into the shell through a ragged hole. It lurched and slid from sight as he swooped higher.

Flames leaping! Havoc blazing in the night. The chaos of attack rending the earth. Again the horrors of war had struck at the heart of the United States!

IN THE brightly-lighted, cabinet-walled inner office of sub-headquarters BD of the United States Intelligence—the chief undercover office in Delaware—Z-7 sat at a desk peering grimly at reports flashing from the communications room. He rose quickly as Operator G-4 entered. The agent's face was white, his lips dry, his eyes still reflecting the horror he had seen descend upon the great Warwick Works.

"Report, Chief!" he exclaimed. "We captured the captain of the Hidden Hundred and—his men got him away from us. But anyway, we made a prisoner of one of his lieutenants."

Z-7 ordered grimly: "Bring that man into the next office!" As G-4 withdrew, he touched the cam of the desk dictaphone and gave another snapping command: "Get the lie detector ready for immediate use!" He rose, strode to a connecting door, paused as another opened. His black eyes glinted at the young man who entered—Operator 5.

"You've come at an opportune moment," the Washington chief declared grimly. "We have taken one of the Hidden Hundred prisoner. I'm going to get the truth out of him—the truth about the identity of his leader!"

JIMMY CHRISTOPHER'S eyes darkened. "Chief, I think we may thank the Hidden Hundred that the Warwick Works were not destroyed completely—and blame the Intelligence for most of the destruction that was accomplished."

Z-7 snapped: "What? Blame the Intelligence for what happened tonight?"

"Perhaps," Jimmy Christopher declared, "it might have been avoided if the Hidden Hundred had been allowed to complete its work!"

Quietly Z-7 asked: "You sympathize with the Hidden Hundred, don't you, Operator 5? Perhaps that is very significant—a fact I should not be happy to have the Secretary of State learn."

"I am always willing to take the consequences, Chief," Operator 5 answered quietly, "of sympathizing with men who risk their lives in the service of their nation while that same nation hunts them as outlaws."

Z-7 strode stiffly into the adjoining office; and Operator 5 followed. They paused just inside, gazing at a man standing in the center of the room. He was garbed in grimy overalls. In spite of the greasiness of his face, he was easily recognizable. A pang of icy dismay coursed through Operator 5's heart—for this man was X-27, judged the most courageous, the most loyal in the Hidden Hundred.

In this room, X-27 stood a prisoner while the guns of men who had once been his comrades kept turned upon him. He gazed at Jimmy Christopher, but no betraying flicker shone in his grim eyes. Operator 5 felt profound admiration for him—the first of the Hidden Hundred to be captured by the Intelligence. He did not flinch as Z-7 stepped forward.

"Knowing you from your past service," the Washington chief began quietly, "I presume that you refuse to confess anything concerning the Hidden Hundred?"

"I do, sir!"

"You will not identify your leader?"

"I would prefer to die, sir, than tell you his name."

Z-7 declared grimly: "I respect you for that—but I cannot accept that stand. You *will* divulge the name of your captain— though you refuse to speak it. You understand, I believe, the operation of the lie detector?"

The face of X-27 went white. Z-7 gestured two men toward him. One led X-27 to a chair. The other brought a table bearing the ingenious device by which the prisoner's uncontrollable reflexes were to be tested. Deftly, the Intelligence psychiatrist affixed the sphygmomanometer above X-27's brachial artery. Quick squeezes of the bulb brought air pressure over that point. Delicate needles, poised to trace their movements on drums of smoked paper, were adjusted. When the preparations were completed—preparations watched with cold dread by Operator 5—Z-7 spoke quietly:

"You realize this device inflicts no pain. It merely records your varying systolic blood pressure, which is a reliable indicator of the strength of the heartbeat. This, in turn, varies according to the amount of nervous effort made by you when answering my questions. If you attempt to lie to me, you will be forced to make a nervous effort to do so, and the fluctuating systolic pressure will be marked on the chart. The lie detector is absolutely unbeatable. Now, do you still refuse to confess your leader's identity?"

"I do!" X-27 blurted. He peered around warily at the men who were still holding their guns on him; but his eyes avoided Operator 5. "Your machine will not help you!"

"WE SHALL see." Z-7 shifted, so that he could watch the wavering needles on the smoked drums. They were tracing a vibrating line which indicated almost normal heartbeat. He asked, gently, eyes upon the traced white waves, "You are, of course, a member of the Hidden Hundred?"

"Yes." X-27 declared it proudly; and the needles did not waver from normal.

"You know who your comrades in this organization are?"

"No." Now the needles jumped, indicating increased strength of heartbeat—nervous effort. The irregular waver betrayed instantly that X-27's answer was a falsehood. "I know none of them!" and the needle jerked again.

"You do not, then, know who your leader is?"

"No!" *Lie!* the indicator announced.

"Have you ever seen his face?"

"No!" *Lie!*

"Is he," Z-7 demanded gently, "one known to me by another identity?"

"I don't know!" *Lie!*

"Three times you have not told the truth. You do know your leader! He is known to me! You can't defeat this machine. That's the truth, isn't it?"

Slowly X-27 admitted: "Yes," and the indicators of the lie detector confirmed his statement.

Z-7 bent close, while Jimmy Christopher watched with cold apprehension, with dread weighting his heart. "Is that man—the leader of the Hidden Hundred—myself, Z-7?"

"No." *Truth.*

"Is he ex-Operator Q-6—John Christopher?"

The lips of X-27 pressed tight.

"Is he—?"

Z-7 hesitated, the name of Operator 5 on his tongue. Jimmy Christopher knew that with a dread certainty. X-27 realized it with terror shining in his eyes. The little wavering needles on the drums moved rhythmically, ready to inscribe their uncanny signature to a death warrant for Jimmy Christopher.

"Is he—?"

Suddenly X-27 whirled from his chair. The rubber tube attached to him snapped free. He struck savagely at the operator behind him. He spun half away, both hands clamped on that man's gun. As others crowded after him, he lurched against the wall; and in the swift confusion of the office, a blasting shot sounded.

The report shocked every man in the room motionless.

Against the wall, X-27 braced himself. The gun trembled in his fingers and dropped. Bright red flowed upon his overalls as he plunged to the floor. Z-7 moved quickly toward him, grasped his shoulder, turned him so that the bright light glared down in his lax face. The Washington chief straightened, hands curled into fists, to speak a whisper:

"Dead!"

Operator 5 stood rigid, chilled with dismay and admiration, looking upon a man who had paid his life to keep the secret of a comrade. On his breast, X-27's own blood formed the red badge of courage.

CHAPTER 6
GOLDEN DOOM

IN THE secret black room, through the shine of a dim glow, the leader of the Hidden Hundred spoke quietly to the corps of skull-masked men who faced him.

"Comrade X-27 chose death rather than to betray our secret. His is an example of courageous self-sacrifice which we must strive to emulate. Let us work together tirelessly, without fear, in the name of our cause—so that X-27 will not have died in vain."

The solemn tones echoed into a reverent hush. Slowly the light dimmed down. The silent men heard the gentle rustle of draperies, and knew that their captain had vanished.

Operator 5, with slow step, walked quietly into the little room which served as his headquarters. When he opened the door Tim Donovan sprang alertly from a chair. Another skull-masked figure followed Jimmy Christopher in. They removed their masks and regarded each other gravely—Operator 5 and John Christopher.

"We're facing an almost hopeless job, Dad. Yet, for the sake of X-27, we must not give up hope."

"You have never failed yet, son," ex-Operator Q-6 declared staunchly. "You will not fail this time."

"Gee, Jimmy!" Tim Donovan exclaimed. "It's a double-edged plan—destroying our military stores, after we've paid for them in gold. It keeps the United States helpless—and if the people find out that our gold reserve is melting away, it will mean revolution!"

"Exactly, Tim," Operator 5 declared. "The United States has awakened at last to her dangerous position in regard to war supplies. Too late—much later than other nations. It is leaving us helpless in an emergency. We may never be able to save ourselves."

He sat at his desk, unlocked a steel drawer, and removed folded documents from it. Among them were the photostatic reproductions of the fingerprints he had taken from the gold gun of the master in the golden mask. Now he reread material he had selected from the voluminous files of the War Department:

Bradshaw, Rederick, Major.

Subject: Court-martial under charges of violating Section 96, Articles of War.

On May 20, 1918, at Sissonne, France, Major Rederick Bradshaw was arrested by operatives of G-2 and charged with dealing with the enemy. Specific charges listed his intimacy with a woman known as Gerga Branda, a known secret agent of the German Espionage Office. Court-martial, conducted at Sissonne on May 25, disclosed circumstances which left no doubt of Major Bradshaw's guilt. Attached is a complete transcript of the testimony.

Summation: Through his infatuation with Gerga Branda, Major Bradshaw agreed to pass United States military secrets to the German Espionage Office. In order to avoid suspicion, payments to him by the enemy were made in gold. A store of gold, hidden in Major Bradshaw's quarters, became damning evidence against him, since he was unable to explain its source satisfactorily. Major Bradshaw was sentenced to death.

Throughout the court-martial, his attitude was one of contempt. Upon pronouncement of the sentence, he denounced the court with almost insane anger, swearing retribution and declaring that he would somehow destroy the name of the United States as the official court-martial had destroyed his. While he was being taken from the court, in a burst of mad desperation, he escaped custody.

Succeeding in eluding pursuit, he made his way under cover of darkness to the base of the 96th Pursuit Squadron, stationed near Sissonne. He waited until dawn, when Flight A was placed on the line in readiness for a dawn patrol. All combat units along the sector had been warned to look for him. At an opportune moment, Major Bradshaw rushed to the waiting planes, and ordered Lieut. Brice Rodgers from his Spad. He used force to empty the pit and in his mad anxiety took Lieut. Rodgers' gun and shot Rodgers dead.

This act was seen by other pilots on the field, and Bradshaw was recognized. He rushed off the field in Rodgers' Spad, pursued by Flight A of the 96th. It was a black, foggy morning, but the chase was hot. Bradshaw turned his guns upon the men following him, and an air battle took place. Bradshaw was seen to plunge down behind the German lines.

After sunrise, a German plane flew low over the field of the 96th and dropped a message. It read: "Major Bradshaw crashed in flames, perished with his plane. With the compliments of Richthofen." The Germans, not knowing the circumstances of Bradshaw's court-martial and escape, made the error of honoring him like a flyer killed in action.

Weeks later, upon the advance of the Allied Army in that sector, a grave was found, marked with a broken propeller, bearing the name of Bradshaw and bearing the date of May 25. His death is recorded as of that date.

The report was signed by the Adjutant General of the Department of War.

OPERATOR 5 murmured: "Killed eighteen years ago—yet alive today. Dead—yet fulfilling his vow of vengeance upon the United States! Richthofen could not have realized it, but this was a trick of Bradshaw's to make himself appear to be dead, and all these years he has been planning to strike back. He's striking in a way that threatens the very existence of the country!"

"Yet Bradshaw cannot be acting alone in this plan, Jimmy," John Christopher declared. "He has vast resources behind him—great power."

"You're right," Operator 5 agreed. "He has—"

He tightened alertly as a light flashed above the desk. Its blue gleam signaled that a secret button had been pushed at the hidden rear entrance of the headquarters. Quickly he reached to a contact beneath the desk and pressed it. Beyond the room, an electric lock clicked free.

He rose, strode to a door, listened. Again he pressed a secret contact and again a bolt withdrew magnetically. He opened the way, peered in astonishment into the black cubicle. A girl hurried out of it—Diane Elliot.

"Good Lord, Di!" Operator 5 exclaimed. "You shouldn't have risked coming here!"

"I had to, Jimmy!" the girl blurted. "I've got a lead—an important lead. I've got to see it through."

She entered the office of the captain of the Hidden Hundred eagerly. Operator 5 closed the door, his blue eyes flashing from her face to Tim Donovan's.

"Both of you," he declared quietly, "helped more last night

GRECKOW   RUFFOLO

HOSTS OF THE FLAMING DEATH

MAJOR REDERICK BRADSHAW

than I can ever tell you. Except for you, Di, thousands might have died in the Warwick Works. Tim, all those buildings would have been completely destroyed if you hadn't directed the bomb attack that sank the sub. Service in the name of the Intelligence—and yet, if you were ever caught!" His voice faded on a note of dread.

"I simply refuse to be afraid, Jimmy Christopher," Diane declared. "I'm with you all the way on this, and you know it. I want to help, no matter what the consequences might be."

"That goes for me, too, Jimmy!" Tim Donovan exclaimed.

John Christopher declared grimly: "I never expected to find myself fighting the Service I've given most of my life to, son, but I'm proud of you and I'm backing you to the limit."

"With that loyalty behind me—with men like X-27 at my side—we *must* succeed!" Operator 5 exclaimed. He turned, asked the girl quietly: "You've got a lead, Di? What is it?"

"A lead," the girl declared, "which proves that the Urakian Ambassador is in the thick of this intrigue, Jimmy!"

Her statement brought a chill to Operator 5's heart. This European power was one which was engaged in a grim battle with the United States over world trade. Her depreciated currency was forcing dangerous inroads into the commerce of the nation. Able, by means of her financial manipulation, to buy raw material, manufacture it, ship it to the United States, and sell the goods at prices far below the cost of manufacture here, she was exerting subtle destructive forces.

ALREADY GROUPS of United States factories had been forced to close down because of the murderous competition. Thousands had been thrown out of employment. Urakian goods were flooding the United States markets in even greater quantities than products of Japanese manufacture. The situation was terrorizing industry in this country, for it was a force counter-acting all the efforts of the administration to promote recov-ery. Diane Elliot's statement was a startling hint that Urakia's operation had extended even farther than this nation dreamed.

Quickly Jimmy Christopher asked: "How do you know the Urakian Ambassador is involved, Di?"

"My boss sent me to him today for an interview," the girl explained. "I had to wait for him in his study at the Urakian Embassy. I noticed ink-marks on his blotter and tried to deci-pher them. It was just something to pass the time at first, but I saw that a signature had been blotted on that sheet again and again. It wasn't Greckow—the Ambassador's—name or the name of anyone connected with the embassy. It was—Haigh!"

"What!"

"Haigh, Jimmy—the name of the British Ambassador! Grec-kow himself had written it. It means that Greckow is a lieu-tenant of the man in the gold mask, using the name of Haigh as a cover."

Jimmy Christopher's eyes sharpened darkly. "A true lead, Diane—one of the most valuable we've had! I'm going to follow that up at once!"

He strode to the door, signaling Tim Donovan to follow. On the sill he paused, his lips pressed tight in thought. "This plan has been months in the building. I saw hints of it months ago—strange actions centering around American gold shipments from all over the world—and now we know that precious metal is going to be used to destroy us!"

Quickly he left the secret office, followed by the eager Irish lad. They descended into the cellar; they passed through a hidden door and came into the adjacent house. Presently they emerged from a doorway half a block distant. They entered a nearby garage together; Operator 5 turned his sleek roadster toward the street on which the Urakian Embassy was located.

He drove without speaking, swiftly; he drew to the curb on the quiet street within sight of the imposing building. Thoughtfully he studied it; then he settled down in the seat. Tim Donovan's eyes were a gnawing question, and Operator 5 answered it with:

"A period of watchful waiting, Tim."

THE BOY'S gaze brightened. "It's been a long while since you showed me a new trick, Jimmy. The last time you performed one with colored ribbons, and you said you had some others like it. How about it?"

"Okay, Tim!" Operator 5 laughed. "I'll show you something that'll keep you guessing." He drew a leather case from his pocket, opened it, and removed three small cardboard tags. He passed them to Tim. The boy examined them eagerly as he explained:

"They're ordinary shipping tags, you see, except that one is red, one blue and one yellow. Look them over and make sure that except for their colors they're identical. Yet—like the trick with the ribbons, Tim—I'll show you that I can tell them apart by the sense of touch alone!"

The boy blinked. "You were able to tell the ribbons apart, when you were blindfolded, because they were of slightly different lengths, but these tags are exactly the same size and weight and everything. I'll bet you can't do it!"

"Then let's go!"

Operator 5 turned his head away, closed his eyes tightly. Tim Donovan selected one of the tags and placed the others in his pocket. "Here you are, Jimmy," he said, and put the third into Operator 5's fingers. Eyes still tightly shut, Jimmy Christopher placed the tag behind his back, and promptly announced, "It's the blue one."

"That's right!" Tim exclaimed in amazement.

Operator 5 repeated the trick quickly, several times, and in each instance divined the color of the tag correctly. Completely mystified, Tim begged for the secret. Jimmy Christopher chuckled as he explained:

"Very simple, Tim. You didn't examine the tags quite closely enough. There *is* a difference between them that tells me at once which is which. Notice, now. Here at the tapered end of the tag is the eyelet through which the cord passes. That's an ordinary part of such tags. The eyelet is strengthened by two little circles of paper. They're the same on all the tags, except in one slight particular.

"Notice that the reinforcement on one side of the yellow tag can be moved. It's loose. Notice that on the blue tag *both* reinforcing circles are loose, that is, one on each side. And on the red tag, *neither* of them is loose. There you are. All you need to do is feel the looseness of the little circular reinforcements when you have the selected tag behind your back!"

"Gee, I missed that!" the boy exclaimed. "That's a slick one!

I can make a set of tags like these myself simply by loosening the reinforcements in the right way with a razor blade, can't I?"

"Certainly, Tim—and paint them with watercolor. I spoke of other tricks just like it. There's a whole series of color divination tricks that can be worked together. There's one with varicolored marbles that I'll explain to you later if I haven't time now—and one with colored matches. That's a slick one, and very easy. Here we go."

Operator 5 unlocked a compartment beneath the seat of the roadster, while watching the Urakian Embassy closely, and from it removed four small boxes of safety matches. He showed them to Tim one by one, pointing out that in each box the sticks of the matches were of a different color. In one box they were red, in another black, in another white, and in the fourth blue. He handed them all to Tim and explained:

"This time I'll be able to tell which one you select by the sense of hearing. All of the boxes are partly empty and they rattle when shaken. Try it for yourself first, then hand me one without letting me see it."

Tim experimented carefully. He held each box, shook it, intently listened, and tried to detect some subtle difference in the sound made. Alert as he was, he was forced to conclude that they all made exactly the same rattling noise when he shook them. Already mystified, he selected one of the boxes while Operator 5 waited with eyes closed, handed it over.

Jimmy Christopher placed it behind his back and rattled it. He handed it to Tim—who covered it with his hand—pondered, and announced: "Red."

"Right again!" the boy exclaimed. "You've certainly got keen ears! I can't tell the difference. I bet you can't do it again!"

But Operator 5 repeated the feat five times with complete success. Each time, Tim became more mystified. At last, with a laugh, Jimmy Christopher gave the surprisingly simple explanation.

"The sound doesn't matter at all—they all rattle exactly alike. But, when I have the box behind my back, I simply open it and remove one of the matches. I conceal that match in my fingers when I return the box to you. I open my eyes while you hide the box, seem to be puzzled, but in reality get a glimpse of the match in my fingers. It's very simply done."

"Doggone!" Tim exclaimed. "I never suspected it, Jimmy! Gee—I try to find some good tricks to do myself, but you have the best ones I've ever seen—the most mysterious and the simplest to do."

"THANKS, TIM! Operator 5 again scanned the black entrance of the Urakian Embassy. "There's a car drawing up to the door now. It's the official machine—it may mean that something important is up."

"Jimmy, will Z-7 get more suspicious by your staying away from WDC-13?" the boy asked anxiously. "You're taking a terrible risk."

"I'll check on that, Tim," Operator 5 answered; and as he watched the shining car waiting in front of the embassy, he reached beneath the dash to click the switch of the radio installation. He brought a handset from a compartment—an instrument containing both transmitter and receiver, like a French telephone—and when the tubes heated, he clicked a distorter into the circuit and spoke softly.

"Calling WDC-13. Operator 5 calling WDC-13 and Z-7."

Almost immediately, an answer came through the ether from the secret headquarters of the Intelligence, where wireless operators were continually on duty. "Picking you up, Operator 5. Connecting Z-7 now. Stand by."

A moment later the chesty tones of the Washington chief followed: "Z-7 speaking. Operator 5? I've been trying to locate you!"

A pang of apprehension pinched Jimmy Christopher's heart as he repeated: "Trying to locate me, Chief? Are there special orders?"

"Urgent orders!" Z-7 snapped. "I have had a telephone call from the White House. The President has asked to see you—he is waiting for you now. Report to him immediately!"

Operator 5's nerves tightened as he clicked the switch and again peered at the official Urakian car. "I've got to abandon this lead, Tim," he declared, "It's up to you now, old-timer—to follow that car."

"I'll do it!"

"I'll have to use this roadster. Try to get yourself a taxi before that car leaves, or you'll be left stranded. Report back as quickly as possible."

"Okay, Jimmy!"

The Irish lad slipped quickly from the roadster. Operator 5 saw him move out of sight in the shadows. Tim was easing toward the intersection in search of a cab when Jimmy Christopher meshed gears. He pulled away, turned a corner sharply, and sped away—his destination the historic dwelling on Pennsylvania Avenue.

Tim Donovan watched Jimmy Christopher swerve out of sight, and, eager to find a taxi, he started to move away; but a movement behind him—a sudden flare of light—stopped him short. He saw the door of the Urakian Embassy opening, glimpsed the face of the man who stepped out and recognized Ambassador Greckow.

In dismay, the boy was obliged to abandon his search for a cab. Realizing that to attempt to follow the official car afoot was hopeless, he darted toward it through the shadows. On the stoop, the Ambassador had paused, speaking to the man who stood in the doorway. Judging hastily that Greckow was intending to use the car alone—seeing that no chauffeur was at the wheel—Tim Donovan sprang to its far side.

He saw that the car had no trunk and no spare tire on the rear—nothing to which he could cling. His mind flashed lightning—and his heart sped when he saw the Ambassador begin descending the steps. Swiftly, because no other opportunity afforded itself, he opened the rear far door of the car and ducked in. He closed it silently, huddling down behind the front seat as the door near the driver's wheel opened.

AMBASSADOR GRECKOW entered, closed the door. Tim's heart beat heavily with dread because Greckow made no move to start the car. He was waiting. Presently footfalls sounded on the sidewalk. A shadow passed across the windows.

Greckow, peering at the man who paused beside them, growled: "Get in, Ruffolo—quickly! We have no time to spare!"

"One moment, sir," the man named Ruffolo answered quietly. "It is well you put me to watching the Embassy from the outside. You have—though you are not aware of it—another passenger!"

"What?"

"Back there!"

Tim Donovan scrambled up frantically. As he reached to thrust open the far door, the nearer opened swiftly. Strong hands snatched at his clothing, dragged him back. He fought with wild, silent fury as Ruffolo crushed upon him, pinioning him down. He kicked, scratched, sobbed in his desperate efforts to free himself—and suddenly he went limp.

The Ambassador from Urakia, gripping an automatic, swinging over the back of the seat, had smashed the weapon forcibly against Tim Donovan's head. The Irish lad dropped lax, unconscious, with the hands of Ruffolo still clamped on him.

"A boy! Who is he?"

"This boy is the unofficial assistant of Operator 5, sir."

"Good God! It means that Operator 5 suspects us! He has linked me with—!" Greckow broke off. "Ruffolo! What can we do?"

"We have no time to waste," Ruffolo answered coolly. "Taking him into the Embassy would be unwise, sir. There is a better place at our destination. I suggest that we proceed—and take him there."

"But if Operator 5 traces him!"

"Not even Operator 5 will be able to trace him, sir. Not even

Operator 5 will be able to find this boy—until he is discovered floating dead in the Potomac."

The Ambassador blanched, but his eyes grew grim with merciless determination. He stamped on the starter, sent the car spurting from the curb. It wound deep into the darkness of a lonesome, outlying section of the capital—and all the while Tim Donovan lay as if already dead....

CHAPTER 7
MISSION OF DESTINY

THE SECRET SERVICE men posted at the gate of the White House passed Operator 5's roadster with a glance. When he entered the famed East Wing, the President's Secretary greeted him anxiously. He was conducted at once to the door of the Chief Executive's study.

Jimmy Christopher was no stranger in the White House. He had been summoned here into conference many times. Now, as he entered the quiet room where the President handled the executive power of a great nation, he smiled. The kindly-faced, gentle-mannered man at the great carved desk rose, extended his hand.

"I am delighted to see you again, Operator 5," he said with the sincere charm that characterized him. "I will never forget your services to the country in the past. I realize that the Secretary of State feels a certain enmity toward you, and protests against your operations, but I have chosen to override his objections now because I esteem you highly. I pride myself on being a judge of men, and among all the men of the Intelligence, I have no hesitation in selecting you for a special mission of vast importance."

"Thank you, sir," Operator 5 said.

"It is a very dangerous mission; it demands the utmost care—all the skillful handling you are capable of giving it. You have never faced a more important detail, Operator 5. Are you willing to undertake it?"

"Of course," Operator 5 promptly answered.

"Knowing," the President queried solemnly, "that failure or bungling will have one inevitable result—to plunge the United States and the entire world into war?"

Operator 5's face paled as he realized the quiet import of the President's words. He answered softly: "I will do my very best, sir!"

"I am not exaggerating in the slightest," the President declared gravely. "The failure of this move will force war upon the United States, embroil us in a horrible conflict that may destroy the whole world."*

"I understand fully, sir. And the success of this mission must rest in the hands of one man?"

"One. You, Operator 5."

The Chief Executive studied the clean-cut face of Jimmy

* AUTHOR'S NOTE: "The next war, if it comes, will mean the end of civilization. We shall return to the tenth century. It may last only two days, but in that short time, the great cities of Europe will have been wiped out; the world will be in chaos; plague and famine will remove the survivors of the green cross gas." John Bayliss in *Everyman,* London, May 18, 1934.

Christopher as he weighed the words he was about to speak. They sat alone in the study, two men whose paramount thought was the welfare of the United States.

The President continued: "You well know that without certain vital materials we will be helpless in time of war. If we neglect to store them up, in time of peace, a blockade or an embargo in time of war might force defeat upon us. Even if this did not occur we would be endangered by any belligerent's declaring our shipments of such supplies to be contraband."

"Certainly, sir."

"Therefore, we began our secret plan of storing up such supplies in time of peace. We found that everything we needed was controlled by a powerful syndicate. We were forced to buy through that syndicate, and to contract to pay gold. An unwritten clause of the agreement stipulated these gold payments would be made later, with interest, but this clause was promptly broken. Gold has been withdrawn from our Treasury in appalling quantities while we were unable to stop the leak. Unwittingly, and through crooked international maneuvering, we have placed ourselves in a situation so dangerous that our absolute destruction may result."

OPERATOR 5 studied the Chief Executive's sharp eyes alertly. The President continued: "It is a fact known only to a few of the highest officials of the government that while our secret military program is almost completed, our gold reserve has dwindled to the lowest point in recent history. It is a situation which, if it becomes known, will plunge the United States into disaster. It will start a race of currency depreciation all over the world which will lead to inevitable financial chaos and complete world breakdown."

"Is it a certainty, sir?" Operator 5 demanded.

"Yes!" the President stated. "You know of the dangerous currency operations of the world since the great war. France depreciated the franc to one-fifth its former value. Germany depreciated the mark from twenty-four cents to zero. Since then, Japan has depreciated the yen, Great Britain the pound, Belgium the belga, the United States the dollar. At the moment, the world is in a state of precarious suspension, with a few nations striving to maintain a gold basis—France, Switzerland. If depreciation begins again, it will become an avalanche of havoc."

"I understand, sir!"

"The United States remains the financial cornerstone of civilization. If we crumble, the whole world collapses. Now, if the world learns that the United States' gold reserve has been seriously diminished, that collapse will come. The secret within our Treasury walls is the most dangerous one in the world. We are faced with two absolute necessities, unless we wish to see the whole world destroyed and the United States with it.

"First, we must keep our condition the strictest of all secrets. Second, we must get that gold back into our Treasury."

"And you are revealing this secret to me, Mr. President," Operator 5 asked, "because you wish to give me the task of returning that gold?"

"Yes. It is possible to get it back in only one way—to seize it secretly!"

"What?" Jimmy Christopher exclaimed. "Take it away from its present holders without the world's knowing?"

The President's grave, glittering eyes were an affirmative answer. "That gold left our Treasury not only because of a broken agreement—but because of outright crookedness on the part of the syndicate!"

Operator 5's eyes widened. "But to attempt to return the gold—to seize it!"

"Therein," the President pointed out, "lies the great danger. To seize that gold by force will constitute an act of war. It will plunge the whole world into conflict. In only one way can we avoid that catastrophe—and get that gold back without open aggression—seize it secretly! That, Operator 5, is the task I am putting into your hands!"

OPERATOR 5 sat speechless, appalled by the magnitude of the President's special orders. "In brief," the Chief Executive continued, "we are striving to recover loot from a ring of international robbers. Unless we succeed in doing so, the United States will crumple and the whole world will collapse with it."

"You have information as to where this gold is, and how it might be transported back, Mr. President?"

"All the gold has been transported across the Atlantic. It is now in the vaults of the syndicate in Switzerland. We know its precise location. As to how we might get it back—the most precious store of gold in the world—the means are strictly up to you. There is one lead, one opportunity—a shipment of gold which has just now left our shores, which is on its way across the sea to the syndicate's secret vaults at this moment."

Operator 5 listened intently while the President explained. He heard all the details and received from the Chief Executive's hand a report in code containing the essential information. He slipped it inside a secret pocket, rose as the President offered his hand.

"Operator 5, you must use the utmost care. There are political enemies of mine who, if they learn of this fact, will use it to crush my administration, unmindful that at the same time they would also crush the nation. There are hundreds, even thousands, of prominent men in this country whom we cannot trust if they learn of it, because they have yielded to subtle diplomatic bribery by foreign nations. Until that gold is returned to our Treasury, the revelation of that secret can mean nothing less than national destruction."

Operator 5 seized the President's hand. With firm, quick stride he left the White House. He drove directly to that section of the capital in which the secret Intelligence headquarters WDC-13 lay. There, entering the inner office, he confronted Z-7. He found the chief tight-nerved, anxious.

"The President," Z-7 said gravely, "has given this mission to you over the protests of the Secretary of State because he has faith in you."

"I will do my utmost, Chief," Jimmy Christopher declared firmly. "Has any report come from Tim Donovan?"

"None."

Operator 5's eyes darkened. "I'm going to draw up a plan of action at once, Chief, to follow the President's orders. No time must be wasted. If any report comes from Tim, may I have it at once?"

Z-7 promptly sent orders to the clattering communications room. At his desk, Operator 5 worked quickly, carefully, building up a scheme of action on the success of which the fate of a nation rested: Now and again he paused, worry darkening his eyes. From Tim Donovan, as long minutes passed, there came no report—and the weight of anxiety in Operator 5's heart became ever heavier as time went on....

SWIRLING LIGHTS, the tom-tomming of a drum, a numbness of pain, filled the brain of Tim Donovan. The tough Irish lad felt himself roughly dragged, dropped onto a couch. He peered up into blinding light as consciousness returned to him—and saw a blear of motion.

The vicious blow had rendered him senseless for long minutes. The drumming in his head was the pounding of his heart. As clarity returned, he made out the details of a small room. Two men, who had carried him with tight, evil grins. One of them growled:

"Take it easy, kid. You won't be here long. You can begin counting your minutes."

The other demanded of the first, while Tim brought himself up on the couch unsteadily: "Stayin' with him?"

"Why should we?" Ruffolo's evil grin spread wider. "The window can't be opened, and it's unbreakable glass. The door's steel. There's no way he can get out or even let anybody know where he is. He can think over his troubles alone—think how it's going to feel to die."

"Wait a minute!" the second man exclaimed as they moved toward the door. "That telephone!"

Tim watched Ruffolo turn to the instrument resting on a table in the corner. The espionage agent picked it up, lurched back, tearing the wires from the box. Grinning anew, he strode out of the door carrying the telephone with its dangling cord. "No use of trying to break away or get a message out—you can't do it, kid!" The door closed with a snap.

Tim Donovan pulled himself up grimly. Now that his eyes were clear—though they still throbbed with pain—he examined his surroundings carefully. It was an amazingly well furnished room, a study. He stepped to the one window and saw that Ruffolo had spoken the truth—it was sealed, and the glass was thick and unshatterable. Beyond, the lights of Washington gleamed.

Tim was able to mark his location approximately, but despair gripped his heart. The door was so strong—so firmly fastened— that all his tugging could not move it a fraction of an inch.

Again he peered around, noting an expensive desk, a console radio, many bookshelves, a studio couch. He went to the desk haltingly, tried to open its drawers, found them locked. He recalled Operator 5's orders, "Report back as soon as possible!" and muttered: "If there were only some way!"

He sensed that an important meeting was taking place in this building—a secret conclave presided over by the leaders of the espionage ring. That would be vital information to Jimmy Christopher. The Irish lad peered around grimly, striving to clear his mind, to think of some means of communicating with

WDC-13 and Operator 5. His heart pounded rapidly as his gaze fell on the big radio.

In Jimmy Christopher's workshop he had labored long hours over the intricacies of radio sets, their newest principles and their basic designs. He had built a number of receivers. Under Operator 5's guidance, he had mastered all the complexities of modern radio construction. Now he wondered if, somehow, he could use this radio to communicate out of his prison.

An instrument built only for the reception of wireless impulses—how could he use it as a transmitter? To alter it so that his voice would carry out over the ether—that, he knew, was impossible. But—the loudspeaker, he knew, could be used as a voice pick-up. Operating in reverse, it would originate electrical impulses of the voice like a microphone. If used in that way—!

TIM DONOVAN'S eyes lighted. He switched the radio on, made sure it was in good working condition, then twisted the volume control so that no whisper of sound emerged. He turned quickly to the box of the telephone from which Ruffolo had torn the speaking instrument. Using his thumb-nail, he unscrewed the single bolt that held the cover. Inside, the terminals of the line were fastened. Now using a letter-opener from the desk, he unfastened these, ran them out of the box, and tore the wire free of the tacks holding it to the wainscoting.

This done, he slid the radio away from the wall so that the wires could reach it. He was able easily to identify the detector tube of the set. Working it partway out of its socket, he exposed the prongs. Next he detached the two leads of the voice-coil of the dynamic speaker. Now with four wires to manipulate, he located the output transformer leads of the power tube. Hopefully he connected the telephone wire to this, and the voice-coil leads to the grid and cathode prongs of the detector tube.

Tim Donovan's hope made him breathless while he made the connections. If his plan worked, his voice, actuating the loudspeaker, would send electrical impulses into the detector tube. The audio amplifying unit of the set would strengthen these impulses and send them out over the telephone line. In order to speak and hear alternatively, he knew he would be obliged to exchange the connections each time. He hooked them so that the set-up would receive and waited tensely.

For a long moment, nothing happened, and Tim Donovan's heart sank. Then, electrifying him, quiet tones came from the radio:

"Operator."

With desperate swiftness Tim Donovan exchanged the connections. Leaning close, he spoke into the dynamic speaker. "Central! Can you hear me, central! Can you hear what I'm saying?"

Again he switched the connections. Again, from the loudspeaker the voice from the exchange said: "Operator! What number are you calling, please?"

With caught breath, with heart pounding, Tim Donovan again made the switch and whispered the secret number of WDC-13. He waited an eternity with the connections exchanged again. Then a quiet voice spoke the code salutation of the Central Intelligence headquarters switchboard. Another transfer and Tim blurted:

"Connect me with Operator 5—quick!"

Again he transferred the wires, and a burst of relief came from his lungs when he heard: "Operator 5! Is that you, Tim? Are you calling, Tim?"

"Jimmy!" The boy gasped the name as he made the new contacts. "Listen, Jimmy! I'm speaking through a radio instead of a telephone and I can't hear you while I'm talking! I've been taken prisoner. Ambassador Greckow and some other men have come to a secret headquarters. I don't know exactly where it is, Jimmy, but—listen!"

The eager Irish lad gave directions which placed the building as accurately as possible. "I think that's right, Jimmy! It's higher than any building I can see between here and the Washington Monument! There's a meeting going on now—I'm sure of it! They—they said they're going to kill me, Jimmy!"

The boy switched the contacts again. Out of the radio speaker, the voice of Operator 5 came crisply: "Good work, old-timer! Sit tight! I'm coming!" Then followed the click of a broken connection; and Tim Donovan sagged down, heart hammering, blood rushing hot, grinning with triumph....

CHAPTER 8
SECRET OF DISASTER

L OW IN the air above the capital of the nation a thing like a black cloud floated. It made no sound as it drifted across the night sky, out of the glare of light at the hub of the city. Like a creature of the empty spaces, it slowed and hovered above a building taller than any others in that section.

It was an army observation blimp, and it had swung from its hangar upon a swift mission under the orders of Operator 5. In the lightless gondola he stood, peering down into the wind, while Z-7 and four brother Intelligence men waited tensely beside him. He had swiftly decided upon this subterfuge as a result of Tim Donovan's startling message; and now his mark lay below him.

"That's the building, without a doubt, Chief," he declared. "Are you ready?"

Z-7 exclaimed: "If the Urakian Ambassador is one of this secret organization, we must act with the utmost care to forestall international complications. The Secretary of State has warned us, you must remember, that we are only to observe, to make no move without his specific directions."

"I know, Chief," Operator 5 answered gravely. "His warning applies to the Ambassador, and to any other diplomatic officials involved—but not to known espionage agents. The man in the golden mask may be in that building right now!"

Z-7 asked quietly: "Your plan?"

"I'm going to land on top of that building," Jimmy Christopher declared. He turned and said crisply to the officer at the controls of the balloon: "Down—low—power off."

The craft, outlined black against the black night sky, drifted and dipped. Operator 5 took the handle of a small black case which he had brought with him from WDC-13. As the blimp soughed slowly over the dark roof, he opened the way. A rope ladder unrolled with a slight clatter; its lower end whipped in the wind. Quickly, Operator 5 climbed down it into the openness of space....

At the bottom, while Z-7 watched anxiously, he dangled and dropped. While he poised on the roof, the balloon rose silently, swinging in the wind. Its next move, Jimmy Christopher knew, would be to discharge Z-7 and his men in the street. He waited until it passed out of sight; then he trod carefully, carrying the black case, to the edge of the roof.

Peering over, he saw lighted windows. One on the end of the building he judged, because of its position, to be that through which Tim Donovan had looked to fix the location of the building. He opened the bag, took out a large aluminum hook. To an eyelet of the hook he firmly knotted one end of a slender rope. Fastening the claw to the cornice, looping the strand around his body, he legged over. He hung a moment, then slipped downward toward the lighted window.

Hanging beside it, he peered in. In the room he saw Tim Donovan moving about nervously. The boy had replaced the radio and the telephone wires. A light tap on the pane made him turn in a flash. The boy's eyes widened eagerly and he darted to the window. Jimmy Christopher's gesture warned him as he leaned forward and whispered:

"Jimmy! There's a meeting, now, in the next room. I can hear voices!"

"Good boy, Tim! Watch sharp!" Operator 5 noted that the window was sealed and unbreakable. "Play for time if anyone comes to take you out!"

Quickly Jimmy Christopher climbed hand over hand to the roof. Breathing hard, he transferred the hook to a point on the cornice around the corner of the building. Below, other lighted windows gleamed. Again Operator 5 snagged the rope around his body, and carefully lowered himself. When he stopped, he was hanging high above adjacent roofs; the wind was whistling past him; and he was poised near the edge of one of the windows.

SWINGING HIMSELF slightly, he peered in. A startled breath broke through his lips. In the room beyond, he saw many faces he recognized—the features of men well-known throughout the country. Some were Senators, some Representatives—all of them were political figures of renown. They were talking together, with puzzled expressions on their faces, making indignant gestures. Amazed as he was to discover these public servants in a secret headquarters of an espionage ring, Jimmy Christopher realized that they had one element in common: they were the avowed political enemies of the President and the President's party!

Clinging to the rope, Operator 5 saw the men in the room cease talking and look toward an end of the room beyond his vision. He heard the click of a door-latch, knew someone had entered. There followed a deep silence. Risking discovery, Operator 5 gripped the frame of the window and swung himself so that he could glimpse the newcomer. One glance, and he allowed himself to swing back. It was the man in the golden mask!

While Operator 5 hung outside the window, chilled and puzzled, the strange voice of the man in the golden mask spoke.

Again Jimmy Christopher experienced the uncanny sensation that this was a dead voice speaking across the chasm of the Unknown. The tones of a man who had perished in the flames of a falling war plane eighteen years before were sounding within that room. Even though he realized the report of Major Rederick Bradshaw's death was false, a feeling of supernatural power pervaded Operator 5.

The politicians in the room stared in amazement. Senator Duncombe advanced to demand: "Who are you, sir? Why have we been brought here in this strange way? Why is your face masked?"

The hollow tones answered: "Secrecy is necessary, gentlemen. You have been escorted here by my men—perhaps rather forcibly—so that I can give you a message of the utmost national importance."

Senator Duncombe snapped: "We are honorable representatives of the people. The fact that you persist in hiding your face means that you cannot give your message in good faith."

"I will leave to you, gentlemen," the man in the golden mask declared, "the matter of deciding in what degree of faith my message must be taken. You may verify it from official sources—in fact, I urge you to do so. You are honorable representatives of the people. That is exactly why I have chosen you as my audience, so that you may transmit the message to your constituents. Upon you and upon them now, gentlemen, rests the salvation of this nation."

The notable figures peered uneasily at each other. Senator

Duncombe declared: "Very well, we will hear you—without obligation and without promise."

"Your obligation to your country is enough," the hollow voice of the man in the golden mask retorted. "You are all political opponents of the President. You deem the course he has taken as dangerous, radical, destructive to the nation. I am here to inform you that your fears are well-founded. I urge upon you to demand from the administration a true statement of the condition of our national Treasury.

"You will find, gentlemen, that the financial structure of the country is undermined. We face ruin. Our gold holdings have dwindled so that financial chaos is inevitable. You do not believe me? You stare at me in disbelief? Then question the President! Demand the truth of the Secretary of the Treasury! Insist that you examine the actual gold in our vaults! See for yourself that the treasury of this nation has become an empty shell. That, gentlemen, is a truth you cannot ignore—and my message!"

COLD DREAD struck at Operator 5's heart as he hung poised outside the window. Only a few hours before, the President had warned him of the great danger if the secret of the drained Treasury should become known. Now a man who had sworn to destroy the nation had revealed it to those who would make political capital of it at the expense of the nation's welfare!

The very man who had forced the perilous condition upon the United States had sounded the signal of disaster!

Stunned by the ramifications of the ruthless plan, Operator 5 peered through the pane at the blanched faces of the men in the room. Their eyes turned to the far corner and again a latch clicked. The man in the golden mask had withdrawn; and now the voices of the others rose in confused amazement and terror.

Jimmy Christopher's hand wrapped tight on the rope which supported him; he pulled himself up. Climbing across the cornice he stood in the chill wind. But the coldness centering around his heart was even sharper. He quickly strode across the black roof, careful to make no sound, and paused near the housing of a skylight. He peered down into a dimly lighted hallway, through unbreakable glass sealed in an immovable frame.

Through it Operator 5 saw three men appear. One strode with heavy, quick step—and his face was covered by a mask of golden mesh. To his lieutenants he spoke imperatively in his hollow, ghostly voice, and his words carried up to Jimmy Christopher:

"The boy—make quick work of him now!"

The golden-masked man turned, stepped through a doorway, vanished. The two others started toward the room in which Tim Donovan was held prisoner. Operator 5 shifted quickly, to see them pause near it. One of them brought up a key even as Jimmy Christopher formulated a plan. Deliberately, he slipped his automatic into his hand, pointed it at the glass, and fired.

Four times in quick succession he sent slugs slamming against the broad center pane of the skylight. He knew his bullets would not smash it, but the violent impacts startled the men below. The glass became whitened with countless cracks, though it held, due to the sheet of celluloid vulcanized in its center. Through the misty white, Operator 5 saw the two men whirl, jerk out guns, and aim upward.

Deliberately he leaped. He flung himself heavily upon the

cracked pane and drove his heels against it with all his strength. Though the square did not part, the violent impact bent it, tore it from its sash. It gave way beneath Operator 5 and he plunged down into the lighted hall. As he dropped, he turned his automatic, fired again, swiftly, twice.

His slugs whistled at the two men beside the door. One thudded against an automatic which was even then rising. The other tore through the second man's sleeve, sent him leaping away. Operator 5 dropped back, swiftly, firing again. One of the guns jerked up and roared. Instantly the single bulb in the hallway shattered; darkness closed down.

Operator 5 darted along the wall to the door through which the man in the golden mask had vanished. Twice, deadly fire blasted out of the dark and bullets plucked at him. He gripped a knob, whirled through into bright light, backed with gun leveled—and stared in dismay. There was no other door in this room—yet it was empty!

KNOWING THAT the man in the golden mask must have left through some secret passage, Operator 5 whirled back. A bullet tore at him as he darted again into the hall. His swift, leaden answer brought a pounding sound out of the dark—heels beating down the stairs. He backed warily, slipping the clip from his automatic, lifting another from a secret pocket and clicking it into place. From the front of the building, guttural voices were sounding; quick movements were rustling. Operator 5 hurried to the door through which these noises of retreat came and found it barred.

"Jimmy!" came faintly in the hall; and the call pulled Operator 5 back. In front of the door of the room in which Tim Donovan was imprisoned, he slipped his pack of master-keys from his pocket. Quickly he tried three; the third drew the bolt. Tim Donovan wriggled into the hall and his hot hand seized Operator 5's.

"Are you all right, Jimmy! Gee, I thought!"

"Stand by me, old-timer! The building is surrounded, but—"

Operator 5 hurried away. Knowing that Z-7 and the Intelligence men were on duty in the street, he rapidly searched the floor. Opening locked doors, by means of his master keys, consumed precious moments. He found the rooms, each outfitted as the unit of an efficient undercover headquarters—all empty. Tim Donovan stayed at his side as they hurried down the stairs, continuing the investigation at each landing. The firing of shots on the top floor had signaled an alarm throughout the building; the espionage agents had fled.

Jimmy Christopher reached at last a steel door which barred the way to the street. On the floor lay a crushed hat, a dropped glove, indicating that men had left hurriedly this way. His master-keys again drew the bolt, and he stepped into the cool wind of the street. Startled, he paused, peering around. In the gloom, there was no movement. Operator 5 had expected to see Z-7 and the Intelligence men holding their prisoners here, but the sidewalk was empty.

Quick steps sounded. Out of the darkness, Z-7 approached. Behind him, his men strode. Operator 5, his amazement increasing, declared: "Chief, the leaders of the ring are getting away through a secret exit—it must connect with another building. Send these men to search the streets!"

Z-7 relayed the orders in a crackling voice. The Intelligence operators darted off in the darkness. Operator 5, peering around in bewilderment, asked: "You've taken no prisoners, Chief?"

Z-7's face was dark-lined, his lips thinned. "The first man out of that door was the Urakian Ambassador. Behind him came a dozen of the most powerful men in the country, politically, whose reputations are above reproach. In God's name, what could I do? Make prisoners of men like that? Impossible!"

"Yet those men have certain information which makes them as dangerous as the worst foreign saboteurs that have ever worked against us, Chief!" Operator 5 exclaimed.

"Our hands are tied!" Z-7 protested. "American statesmen cooperating with foreign espionage agents in the name of patriotism!"

Grimly, Operator 5 waited in the gloom, his mind reviewing the desperate predicament he faced. The Intelligence men's search of the surrounding streets, he knew, must be maintained for hours if the capture of the espionage ring leaders could be hoped for. The lieutenants of the masked leader must, he knew, be hiding now in some cleverly hidden warren, reached by the secret door, waiting until the way out was clear. A deep sigh came from Operator 5 as he said:

"Thanks to you, Tim, we know the danger we're facing. The worst crisis we've ever met—and we're forced to stand by helpless!"

OPERATOR 5, a late newspaper tucked under his arm,

entered the imposing office of the Secretary of State. His eyes were a deep, grim blue; his lips were pinched. He paused, facing the stern man at the broad desk. Unflinchingly he returned the Secretary's accusing gaze.

"You sent for me, sir?"

"I did. In any ordinary instance, Operator 5, I should leave the reprimanding of an Intelligence agent to Z-7. This is not an ordinary instance. The situation is so serious that I am obliged to tell you you have precipitated a grave national crisis."

Operator 5 asked quietly: "In what way, sir?"

"Here," the Secretary declared, gesturing to a letter written on heavy note paper, "is a protest from the Urakian Embassy concerning your investigation of Ambassador Greckow. It has brought a severance of diplomatic relations with Urakia—a possible war—to our very doorstep—and you are responsible!"

"Apparently," Operator 5 answered tightly, "you believe the Ambassador's protest has more merit than my investigation."

The Secretary snapped: "This, Operator 5, in the nation's department of peace! You have endangered our peace! The Ambassador has denied any justification for an Intelligence investigation. I am forced to make formal apology."

"Of course, sir," Operator 5 replied bitingly, "you must be most polite diplomatically to this man who is plotting to destroy our nation!"

The Secretary's face went white with wrath. "I am ordering you," he declared, "withdrawn immediately from all connection with this case. If it were not for the fact that the President has entrusted you with a special mission, I should discharge you from the Service. I want you to know that I emphatically disapprove of the President's trusting such a vital matter to your hands!"

Operator 5's eyes blazed. "I am acting with only one motive, sir—the preservation of the safety of the United States. You have every right to rebuke me, and I will follow your orders—but I urge you to take other means of combating the power that is striking at us. If you do not—"

"That, young man, I will determine for myself!"

"Yes, sir!" Jimmy Christopher leaned forward. "We both realize we're facing a desperate emergency, sir. The danger confronting us is all the more threatening because it is intangible. I have tried to do my best to destroy it. Yet the predicament has become so critical that a few words spoken by an American politician will plunge this nation into chaos."

The Secretary demanded: "What do you mean by that?"

Operator 5 unfolded the newspaper he had brought with him, pointed to a black headline. "Tonight, over a nationwide broadcasting network, Senator Duncombe is going to speak. His subject will concern the national financial program. He intends to inform the people of the secret which must be kept at all costs. What, sir, is being done to prevent this—to stop the signal that will mean revolution and panic?"

Stiffly the Secretary answered: "The President and I are striving our utmost to restrain Senator Duncombe, but—. That is all I can say at the moment. I suggest you concentrate on your mission abroad. You're leaving for Europe tonight, are you not?"

"Yes, sir. All my plans are made."

"I trust, then," the Secretary growled, "that you will succeed—that you will not become the direct cause of a new war that will devastate the world!"

Operator 5 paled. He stepped back, and tension thinned his lips as he closed the door....

FROM MILLIONS of radios throughout the nation, an announcer's voice spoke: "Ladies and gentlemen, we call your special attention to an address by Senator Duncombe to begin in exactly one hour. It is of tremendous significance, and we urge the entire nation to listen to this vital, historic broadcast."

The words echoed softly in a sumptuously furnished penthouse in the East Sixties of New York City. A meticulously kept hand turned the switch which silenced the radio. It was the extremely capable one of Crowe, gentleman's gentleman extraordinary of the world-famous photographer Carleton Victor.

It was Crowe's particular idiosyncrasy never to read a newspaper, never to listen to anything on the radio save the finest classical music. His all-absorbing attention in the care of Carleton Victor accounted for it. The walls of this luxurious penthouse were his entire world—in which he was supremely content to give his master the service of a perfect valet. He achieved this with superlative success—and never dreamed that the admirable Carleton Victor was none other than Operator 5.

Victor maintained impressive studios on Fifth Avenue, where the most famous personages in the world came humbly seeking the favor of his work. As a photo-portraitist, Victor had no peer. His signature on a bromoil or a parchment transparency in platinum was a credential valued above all others by those who appreciated modern fine arts. Yet Victor's artistry and Victor's charming personality were convenient covers under which Operator 5 took seclusion.

The ringing of the telephone drew Crowe from the radio. He took up the instrument, heard the voice of Carleton Victor. Immediately he was all dignified attention, though the message which came to him unruffled him subtly.

"I have instructions for you, Crowe," Victor explained. "You are to go at once—protecting yourself from the inclement weather so that you won't catch cold—to the studios of the Universal Broadcasting Company. Wait for me in Studio D on the fortieth floor."

"To a broadcasting studio, sir?" Crowe asked in the same incredulous tone he might have used had he been directed to enter a burlesque show or a hot-dog stand or an asylum for the insane. "Did I understand you rightly, sir?"

"You did, Crowe, indeed," Victor answered with a chuckle. "Do not be misled. I am not going to broadcast. I shouldn't dream of it. I do, however, wish you to wait for me in Studio D on the fortieth floor, where I will soon meet you. You understand that perfectly?"

Very doubtfully Crowe answered "Yes, sir. Very well, sir! I will leave at once, sir." With the air of a martyr, he left the telephone, went into his modest room, and garbed himself against the possibility of catching cold.

When, a few moments later, he emerged from the penthouse, he was wearing a long topcoat, woolen gloves, and gaiters. Above the heavy muffler which he had wound around his chin, his pointed nose quivered with dignity as he set forth to fulfill the strange orders of his master.

Far across the city, Operator 5 had lowered the telephone over which he had spoken as Carleton Victor. The room was one of several which he secretly maintained in New York—unknown even to Z-7—as havens of retreat. He stepped from it into an adjoining room, glanced at his watch. There a score of men were waiting for him. They were members of the Hidden Hundred.

"We leave at once. You have complete directions. In case of capture or other emergency, those who remain must carry out our arrangements. Let me warn you again that this mission tonight is as vital to the safety of the nation as any we have yet undertaken."

The members of the secret band followed him from the room. They trod down carpeted stairs, emerged into the street through a gloomy doorway, went to cars waiting at the curb. There Operator 5 whispered an address: "The New York home of the Secretary of the Treasury. He is there tonight. It is our destination."

AT HIS residence on Fifth Avenue, opposite Central Park, the world-famous industrialist and financier, who had devoted himself unstintingly to the captainship of the nation's finances at a heavy cost to his personal fortune, was pacing the floor in great agitation.

No man in the United States appreciated more keenly the crisis facing the nation tonight. He realized profoundly that Senator Duncombe's message, soon to be broadcast, was a short-sighted political attack which would cause the collapse of public faith in the administration at Washington—revolution, panic, the crushing of the United States! His face, white with appre-hension, lighted with anxious hope as he turned to the ringing telephone.

"The President calling," came over the line; the grave voice of the Chief Executive followed. "The President speaking."

"Mr. President! Have you succeeded in forestalling Duncombe's talk and—?"

"I have not. He is determined to tell the people the very thing that will destroy them—in spite of all the influence I can exert on him. He is thinking no farther than the next local elec-tion—and the destiny of the nation that hangs in the balance! I'm afraid there is little more we can do."

"We've got to stop him!"

"How?" the President demanded. "Our hands are tied. There's no way except by appealing to him, and he refuses to listen. I am going to try once more, but if that last attempt fails, we must prepare to see the nation fall into ruins around us."

"If there is anything I can do, Mr. President—"

"If only you were speaking tonight, reassuring the people that we are still safe—but now it is too late!"

The Secretary of the Treasury lowered the telephone with dread weighing like lead on his heart. He stood, lost to his surroundings, in an agony of anxiety. Then a disturbance in the house startled him. He looked up to see his manservant rush-ing into the library. His eyes widened with alarm as the servant blurted:

"I—I don't know what is happening, sir! Masked men—forc-

132

ing their way in! They have guns! Shall I phone for the police, sir? They—they're coming and—!"

"We're here." The quiet, muffled statement came from a figure which stepped through the doorway at that moment. He was a ghastly apparition. His hands were the claws of a skeleton; his head, a fleshless skull in which live eyes gleamed. In one cadaverous hand he leveled an automatic at the dismayed Secretary of the Treasury.

"All your servants," his muffled voice declared, "are being held. It will be quite useless to attempt to notify the police. The telephone wires are cut, and everyone inside this house will remain a prisoner for the time being. I wish to assure you, sir, that we mean you absolutely no harm."

The startled statesman blurted: "You—you are the Hidden Hundred!"

"I am honored," the man in the skull mask answered, "to be the captain of the Hidden Hundred. Our means may be illegal, but our purpose is above criticism. You too, sir, are surely earnest in your desire to allay the crisis facing us tonight?"

"I would give my life to stop this thing!" the Secretary exclaimed. "But—?"

"Permit us, then," the captain of the Hidden Hundred interrupted suavely, "to commit the unparalleled crime of kidnapping you, sir!"

CHAPTER 9
SKELETON STRATEGY

TONIGHT THE great skyscraper of the Universal Broadcasting Company—towering within a few feet of being the tallest building in New York and the world—was the center of a secret web of intrigue.

Nationally famous radio stars passed under the neon-lighted marquises of the tremendous edifice. Thousands of persons thronged in and out day and night, sightseeing through the scientific marvels, attending programs to which millions listened by air. In studios far above the streets, constructed to make them acoustically perfect, these programs were enacted. The voices of the entertainers flashed over a network of wires, were multiplied by a hundred aerials, were multiplied yet again in countless radio receivers.

In one of these studios tonight, Senator Duncombe was scheduled to speak the words which would send the greatest nation in the world toppling from its financial foundation.

It was located on the forty-fifth floor—a room which appeared to be a comfortable and tastefully furnished library. In its appointments, there was not the slightest suggestion of a broadcasting studio. It might have been part of a sumptuous home, for Senator Duncombe would sit at a desk and speak quietly to a friend seated opposite, as if in the greatest confidence. Yet a microphone concealed in the desk lamp would spread his merest whisper over the United States.

In this room now, as the moment of the broadcast approached, there was only one man—Z-7. He turned quickly as the door opened. Senator Duncombe, florid-faced, nervous, strode into the library followed by four other men. They were Intelligence agents detailed as his bodyguards by the Washington chief. They closed the door, stood with their backs to it as Duncombe strode heavily to Z-7.

"Thank you for the protection," he said acidly. "Especially since you, as much as anyone else loyal to a misguided President, should like to see me silenced tonight."

Z-7's face flushed angrily. "I serve the nation, regardless of political affiliations. It may surprise you to know that the President urged me to protect you carefully tonight. He may protest what you have to say, but he will defend to his utmost your right to say it."

Duncombe bowed mockingly. "Very good—very noble, I'm sure. It's a great pity the President hasn't been as admirable in his handling of the government. You are certain, then, that I am absolutely safe—that I will not be interrupted?"

Z-7 pointed grimly to the window. "You are forty-five stories above the street—unreachable. Every step of the way is protected by my men. You are as safe as it is humanly possible to make you. Now, may I know the reasons for your misgivings?"

SENATOR DUNCOMBE removed a letter from his inner pocket, passed it to Z-7. The Washington chief's black eyes narrowed; the smouldering light in them deepened. He read a laconic, terse message:

Senator Duncombe:

You will not make your address tonight. If you attempt it, you will be silenced. The welfare of the nation demands it.

XI.

"The symbol of the Hidden Hundred," Z-7 said, nodding.

"And this," the Senator declared, drawing another letter from his pocket, "has been received by every member of my party who knows the appalling facts of the President's mismanagement."

Again Z-7 read a sinister message:

Await the result of Senator Duncombe's attempt to broadcast tonight. You must remain silent. Unless you do, his fate will become yours.

XI.

"The others," Duncombe declared, "are intimidated. I am not. That is why I am daring to tell the truth to the whole nation tonight!"

The soft purr of a telephone bell sounded in the room. It was an instrument which was disconnected during broadcasts, available at other moments. Now, as Duncombe answered it, he heard voices which meant an important and special long-distance call was coming through. He stiffened when, at last, he recognized the grave voice of the President of the United States.

"Good evening, sir!"

"Senator Duncombe," the President said solemnly, "I beseech you again to forget party differences—to think only of the welfare of the nation. Silence is our strongest weapon against panic—silence, at least, until the crisis is past. Once we are out of danger, I will not care what you say about me and my administration!"

Duncombe's voice rasped and he spoke pompously, as though repeating phrases from the address he had prepared: "The condition into which you have plunged the Treasury, Mr. President, will force inflation upon us—uncontrolled, destructive. The cause of our welfare cannot be served by silence, because the people must be urged to put a capable man in your place. Otherwise, their savings will be lost, their homes destroyed, their families shattered by panic. It is quite useless, Mr. President. I am going to tell the nation the truth—that's final!"

He crashed the receiver down, his eyes glinting. Z-7 stood motionless, black eyes smouldering. And on the desk, the red hand of an electric clock was twirling away the last few minutes before the broadcast that would spread panic from coast to coast and border to border—a red hand signaling the approach of red terror....

Far below this studio in the honeycombs of the spire, the estimable Crowe approached the Universal Broadcasting Company's marquise. As he turned to enter the chromium and black doors, a man brushed against his side. Startled, Crowe heard a voice murmur: "You'll need this!" and felt something pressed into his hand. He turned in alarm, but the man who had spoken was already lost in the crowd. He gazed puzzled at the envelope he held.

Curiously he read the message it contained:

To the Captain, U.B.C. Ushers:

The bearer of this letter, Mr. Crowe, has had Studio D. Floor 40, placed at his disposal for the evening. Please see that his wishes are fulfilled and that he is undisturbed.

It was signed by a name strange to Crowe—but all-powerful in the studios of the broadcasting system—that of the President of the great radio corporation. Disturbed, yet anxious to follow the instructions of his master, Crowe presented this letter to the black marble desk in the lobby of the great building. Immediately, he was assigned an usher escort. An elevator whisked him to the fortieth floor....

ONCE INSIDE Studio D, the usher himself bowed out. Left alone, Crowe looked about him at strange paraphernalia. There were standard microphones, sound-making devices, a grand piano. In the walls, there were sliding panels of steel, some partly opened on sound-absorbent backing, which were used to vary the "hardness" of the room's acoustics. Crowe, utterly bewildered, lowered himself into an easy chair and waited.

"I think," he said to himself uncomfortably, "that all this is very odd of Mr. Victor."

The man who was Victor to Crowe was, at that moment, standing in another studio on the forty-second floor. A letter—cleverly forged, as was Crowe's—bearing the name of the president of the corporation had placed it at his disposal. As Operator 5 waited, other men entered to join him and stand silent. While one guarded the door, the others affixed weird masks over their heads, strange gloves on their hands.

Secretly here in the spire, as the moment of Senator

Duncombe's speech approached, the Hidden Hundred were assembling under orders of their hunted leader.

A last time the door opened. The man who entered was known as X-13—Operator 5's father. He hurried anxiously to his son, spoke in a whisper:

"Jimmy! Duncombe has notified Z-! The studio is guarded! Trying to stop the broadcast now is hopeless! It can mean only one thing—your capture!"

Grimly Jimmy Christopher declared: "It's a chance I'll have to take, Dad!"

John Christopher exclaimed: "No! I'm afraid of this! Think what it means—Z-7's seizing you as the leader of the Hidden Hundred. It will mean the death penalty for you and it will break Z-7's heart to have to convict you. Think of what you mean to Tim and Diane and me, Jimmy—and don't go through with this wild gamble!"

"I've got to, Dad!" Operator 5 declared.

X-13 seized Jimmy Christopher's hand. "Listen, son. For you to lead the Hidden Hundred tonight is certain to result in disaster for all of us. I want to save you from that. I—my days are numbered. I might die at any moment, because of this bad heart of mine. I—I'm going to Z-7. I'm going to tell him I'm the leader of the Hidden Hundred—and once and for all save you from—"

"You can't do that, Dad!"

"I'd rather face a firing squad than see you do it, Jimmy!" John Christopher cried in torment. "You mean more to the Service

Muffled explosions—followed by groans—sounded as the fumes took effect!

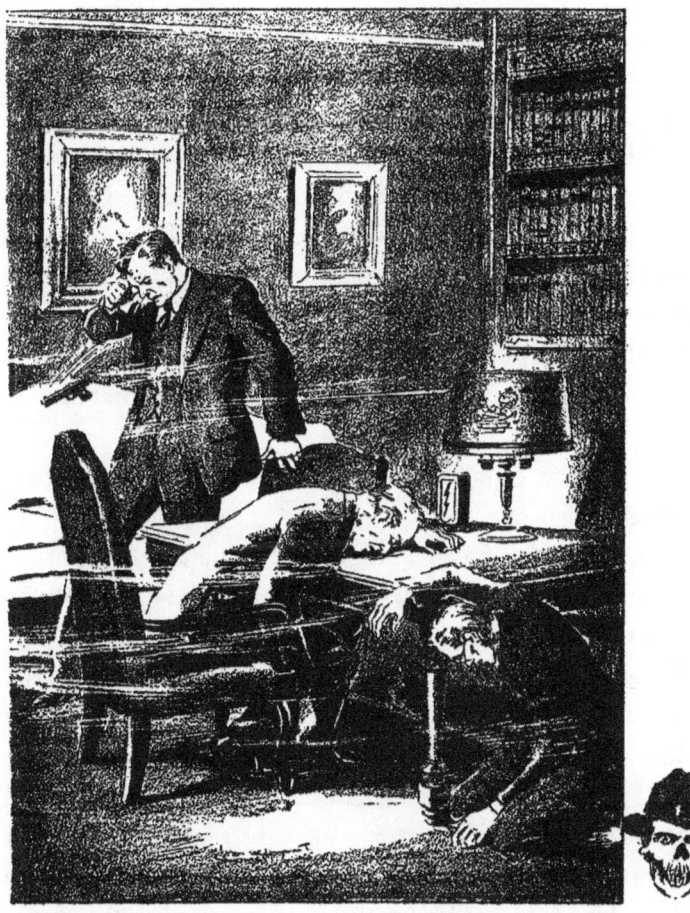

and our country than any other man living. To risk it all—when I might save you from it—!"

"Thanks, Dad." Operator 5's voice was husky as he seized his father's hand. "But I can't let you do that. The risk is mine, and I can't let anyone else assume it. Tonight, a man is going to speak a few words into a microphone—and if he does, the result will be more devastating than an armed invasion. It simply must be stopped and—"

IN THE room a new voice sounded—soft tones issuing from a loudspeaker in the wall. It stated the call-letters of the New York station of the national chain over which Senator Duncombe was about to speak. The announcement marked the hour. Operator 5 snapped to instant attention as a new voice followed:

"Ladies and gentlemen of the radio audience, Senator Duncombe brings you tonight a message of such vital importance—"

Into the flow of fateful words, Operator 5's voice crackled: "Men! Now!"

That moment signaled a program of desperate, swift action, each move of which had been carefully planned in advance by Jimmy Christopher.

The members of the Hidden Hundred rushed out of the studio. At the same instant, other skull-masked men went into action at widespread points in the skyscraper. Ushers were herded aside at the points of guns. Claw-hands gripped the controls of the swift elevators. The cabs manned by human skeletons whirred up through the shafts. Other members of the Hidden Hundred herded up the stairs connecting the studio floors. The signal had sounded!

The claw-hands of the living skeletons gripped gleaming spheres as they crowded onto the forty-fifth floor. In the corridor, Intelligence operators on guard jerked with dismay. As they rushed toward the room in which Duncombe's broadcast was originating, the shining spheres streaked through the air. Hollow coughing sounds followed—muffled explosions. Misty gas flooded up in amazing volume, dimming the lights. Through the fog of stupefying vapor, Operator 5 led his skeletons forward....

They rushed to the door of the library studio, whipped in. A gasp of astonishment broke from Z-7 and the other Intelligence men as the skeletons bounded across the sill into the room. Automatics flicked up, but the gleaming glass-shelled bombs sped through the air and again muffled explosions sounded. Agonized groans followed as the fumes choked the men in the room. At the microphone Senator Duncombe choked—and became silent.

In that mad confusion of vapor and pain, Z-7 sensed quick, desperate movements. He leaped for the open door. He found the corridor clouded with the same suffocating gas. Through the haze, Z-7 saw his men staggering, blinded, helpless. He peered back at the desk at which Senator Duncombe had been talking, saw that the chair was empty. His shout rang sharply:

"Watch the stairs! Take the elevators! Look for Operator 5! Unmask any man you corner and look for Operator 5!"

The announcer rushed as the Intelligence men sped away under Z-7's orders. "The Senator's gone! He's not in the studio! The broadcast is interrupted. In God's name—!"

The purring telephone jerked him back into the room as Z-7 sprang away. Over the line, from another studio, the gasping voice of a program director snapped.

"The Secretary of the Treasury is in Studio A, Floor 44! I've induced him to continue the talk over the same network! An excuse has been made to the audience. It's the best we can do!" IN THE shafts of the great building, elevators were whirring. Through a grille on the ground floor, masked men came rushing, brandishing automatics. Policemen found themselves helpless as the skull-headed men rushed out the main entrance. With them they forced a florid-faced, stocky man who was numb with terror—Senator Duncombe.

Skeleton hands thrust the Senator into a car. A hushed voice warned: "Keep quiet if you want to live!" Gears ground, wheels spun, and a swift sedan whisked the Senator out into the confusion of the streets.

High above, Z-7's frantic orders were still ringing. "Close all stairs—take charge of all cabs! Those men have unmasked—they're getting away! Look for Operator 5!"

Operator 5, at that moment, was bounding through the corridor of the floor five stories below. This move was part of his careful plan. Still masked, he darted to the door of Studio D. He whirled through it unseen by anyone outside, came to a sharp stop, staring at the whitened face of an amazed manservant.

Crowe had been listening to the words issuing from the loudspeaker. He had heard Senator Duncombe abruptly break off, and an announcer's hurried statement that the Senator had become indisposed. Now the ringing tones of a new voice were filling the studio—that of the Secretary of Treasury.

"Our strongest weapon against despair is faith in our President and his administration!"

Crowe jerked up as the man with the skull mask advanced

to him rapidly. "I say!" he exclaimed when the living skeleton seized his shoulders and spun him around.

"Sorry—very sorry!" the muffled voice of the captain of the Hidden Hundred came as Crowe gasped—drawing into his lungs the sweet, thick vapor exuding from a cloth pressed tightly over his nose and mouth.

Crowe's thin knees bent. He sagged to the floor in a deep slumber. The captain of the Hidden Hundred hurriedly bolted the door. From an inner pocket, he drew a compact metal case. Opening it, removing makeup materials, peering into the mirror inside its lid, he jerked off his mask. Swiftly, Operator 5 began to apply pigments and putty to his features, altering them to a startling degree.

Ten minutes later, the door of Studio D, Floor 40, opened, and a thin-faced man with a pointed nose emerged. He was clad in long topcoat, mittens, gaiters, muffler: he was Crowe to the life! He hurried to a cab; and when the grille opened, a hand seized his arm grimly. "Here—who're you?" the voice of an Intelligence operator demanded. "Nobody can get out of here without identifying himself and—"

An usher broke in breathlessly: "This man is all right, sir. I took him to Studio D myself. He had a letter signed by the president of the corporation."

The Intelligence man growled: "All right. He looks like he's scared to death anyhow. An old woman like him couldn't be mixed up in this thing!"

"Thank you, sir! No, sir!" Operator 5 exclaimed in the accented voice of Crowe. A moment later, suppressing a smile, he walked past the irate Z-7 in the lobby and out of the great building.

An hour later, the storm of excitement in the great radio building had subsided. By the aid of their gas-bombs and timed movements, every masked member of the Hidden Hundred had succeeded in escaping. With them Senator Duncombe had gone—as if vanished off the face of the earth. Z-7's search of all the studios had been thorough, and he was forced to the conclusion that the *coup* of the Hidden Hundred had succeeded.

Grimly, the Washington chief hurried to the New York head-quarters, bent on launching a grim search for Senator Duncombe and for the outlaw members of the Hidden Hundred.

Yet, in Studio D, on Floor 40, there was one man even more bewildered than Z-7. As consciousness returned to him, he found himself in a situation utterly new in his experience. He was cold, half-clad, enclosed in a narrow but wide space. It was like a shallow closet, apparently without a door. Utterly bewildered, Crowe sniffed, pushed at the wall in front of him. When, at last, his efforts slid the panel aside, he learned that he had been placed behind one of the sliding doors used to vary the acoustic conditions of the studio.

HE STEPPED into the empty room. On a chair he saw a hat and coat not his own, but quite acceptable to one desperately in need of clothing to shelter him from the inclement weather. On the grand piano he found a note written in the precise script of Carleton Victor. Crowe read it and sniffed again in dismay:

Crowe:

You have inconvenienced me by failing to keep our appointment. Please return to the penthouse at once and prepare yourself for a severe reprimand.

Carleton Victor.

Crowe, wearing the strange hat and coat, emerged from the skyscraper a few moments later. With swift steps, with nose twitching frantically, he hurried off. Never before, he reflected, in all his life had such a strange thing happened to him. Above all else, he thought hopelessly as he hurried, what could he possibly say to Mr. Victor?

The widened scope of Z-7's manhunt had allowed Crowe to slip unnoticed from the building. In the windowless suite of rooms which served as the New York headquarters of the Intelligence, the Washington chief was snapping orders in hope of locating the missing Senator and the captain of the Hidden Hundred. As he worked, reports flashed in to him from scattered points of the city—reports which narrowed his smouldering eyes and drew his grim lips tight.

... NO SIGN OF SENATOR DUNCOMBE... ALL MEMBERS OF HIDDEN HUNDRED IN HIDING... CAPTAIN OF HIDDEN HUNDRED MADE CLEAN GETAWAY....

The communications chief called through the doors. "The President calling!" Z-7 took the message at his desk, heard the Chief Executive say:

"I'm almost ready to thank the leader of the Hidden Hundred for tonight's episode! The Secretary of the Treasury made a magnificent speech. We're safe for the time being—depending on the success of Operator 5's mission. If that boy fails, nothing can save us. He *must* succeed!"

Z-7 muttered, when the connection was broken, "Operator 5!" His suspicions of Jimmy Christopher had strengthened following the *coup* of the Hidden Hundred. "God! If that boy—" He was interrupted by another call from the communications room.

"Radio message coming in, Z-7! Take it on your phone! From the *Messenger,* at sea!"

Z-7 lifted his telephone to hear a voice which sensitive apparatus had picked out of the ether.

"Operator 5 reporting, Z-7. I am safely on my way, aboard the *Messenger!* We are proceeding under full steam!"

Z-7's fingers drummed. "What do you think, Operator 5," he asked slowly, "of the disappearance of Senator Duncombe tonight at the beginning of his broadcast—at the hands of the Hidden Hundred?"

"I think, Chief," Operator 5 answered smoothly, "that the Secretary of State had best realize his restrictions on the Intelligence are forcing the Hidden Hundred into action. I hope he reinstates all discharged men—rebuilds the service to its former strength!"

Z-7's fingers drummed again. "If the Secretary does that, we will have the leader of the Hidden Hundred to thank for it! That man has covered himself tonight very cleverly, but the moment is coming when he'll be unmasked—and doomed!"

"It's inevitable, Chief," Operator 5's voice answered gravely.

"In the meantime," Z-7 declared grimly, "I wish you success on the most important mission you've ever undertaken."

"Thanks, Chief! I'll do my best!"

Z-7 lowered the telephone thoughtfully. His face was white with anxiety, his eyes a sparkling black. He peered again at the terse report on his desk. In agony he muttered: *"Is* Operator 5 that man—*is he?"*

He envisioned Operator 5 crumpling before the barking rifles of a firing squad…!

CHAPTER 10
GOLDEN TRAIL

THROUGH THE night sky, traveling with the speed of sound across the Atlantic, a wireless report came crackling into WDC-13. It bore a symbol which showed that it came from the secret headquarters of the United States Intelligence in Geneva, Switzerland. It was a message for which Z-7 had been waiting through anxious days and nights. Cryptic symbols when it was received, it passed through the codes-and-ciphers room to become an intelligible, terse message:

> … WDC-13… OPERATOR 5 AND MEN ARRIVED SAFELY TODAY… PLAN OF ACTION NOW UNDER-WAY… GSE….

"Plan of action now underway." Only that to signify that Operator 5's strategy had been undertaken—while the fate of a world power poised in the balance of destiny…!

Over the city of Geneva, center of international peace negotiations, a quiet night lay. Here representatives of world powers had frequently gathered for the consideration of treaties and alliances which shaped the history of the world. Here, tonight, agents of the United States Intelligence had come secretly on a mission that would also help shape the course of civilization. And in that crystal, starlit night there hovered a portent of ghastly civilization-destroying war.

Along a winding, mountainous road, a great fleet of lorries was moving. They were mammoth vehicles, carrying weighty loads. Their engines snarled with power as the massive wheels climbed steep grades, turned sharp curves. Each was a traveling fort, built of armor steel, manned with armed guards. Throughout the night, these wheeled giants had been straining over the roads with their ponderous freight.

An unsleeping crew had accompanied them from Marseilles on the long, nerve-straining trek. At that great port, small but amazingly heavy boxes had been transferred from the hold of a trans-Atlantic steamer to these trucks. Up from the sea they had crawled, past the France-Switzerland border. Now, parading within sight of beautiful Lake Geneva, they crawled on their way to the strongrooms which were their destination....

Past a particularly perilous bend, one after another of the elephantine vehicles snorted. Their headlights were dimmed, their crews alert as they neared the end of their long, wearying journey. Except for the dim shine of their lamps, the night lay dark on the curve. Unknown to the drivers and the armed guards, eyes hidden in the darkness watched them—the eyes of agents of the United States Intelligence led by Operator 5!

A swift steamer and rapid transportation by plane across-country from Boulogne had carried Operator 5 to this point before the cargo could come by its longer route. He and his men had brought with them crates of equipment which had passed through the customs-barriers as manufacturing machinery. Posing as American industrial engineers, they had eliminated every possible delay. Now they were ready to undertake a preliminary step in their momentous plan.

Danger had stalked Operator 5 and his men at every step of their long journey. Disguises had courted the chance of exposure and arrest. On a continent of nations fearful of imminent war, where the hunt for spies grew more intense daily, they had risked capture as espionage agents—they had faced every hour the penalty of the captured spy—death before a firing squad. At every frontier they had dared discovery and the failure of their mission; but the shrewd planning of Operator 5 had brought them safely....

OPERATOR 5, hidden with his men beside the road, watched the giant trucks crawl past. Between the vehicles, heavy chains dangled, connecting them all, so that mutual assistance could be given. At the same time, the steel bond assured every driver that the rest of the caravan was safely on the move. At last, the final car in the linked parade appeared chuffing around the bend. Operator 5 gave the signal for quick action....

Four of his men pulled on strong ropes. Beneath the surface of the crushed stone pavement of the road, two heavy blocks moved apart. Loose gravel dropped into the cavity as they were withdrawn. Unseen beneath the gleam of the dimmed head-lamps of the last truck, a barrier opened. Slowly the gigantic vehicle approached it; and suddenly, with a heavy lurch, its front wheels wedged down—immovable.

Swiftly, others of Operator 5's men went into action. Two rushed forward carrying heavy cutters. They bit the keen blades into the chain which bound the last lorry to the one ahead. The link parted; the chain dropped, went rattling up the slope like a disjointed steel snake. Unnoticed by the men in the truck before, the protective connection was broken.

Now guns poked from the vents of the driver's compart-ment and through the steel walls of the truck. The spiteful snap of rifles sounded. The reports were not sharp enough to reach the other trucks through the thunderous snarling of their own engines. The bullets, powerful as they were, were not enough to fell the Intelligence men working with Operator 5. Every square inch of their bodies was protected by bulletproof mesh. Slugs caromed off them as they retreated, sending them stumbling, but except for the shock, they were uninjured.

Immediately the chain was parted, Operator 5 led his other men forward. They darted to a point at the truck's side, out of reach of the guns. Quickly they set up an acetylene tank. Blinding flame leaped from its nozzle as an igniting spark caught. The powerful blade of fire cut rapidly into the steel walls of the truck. The armor plate parted like cheese under a sharp knife.

Rifles spat from the vents, but Operator 5 and his men disregarded them. Once an opening was made, another tank was brought alongside. Its nozzle was thrust inward. A turn of a cock brought a sharp, hissing sound. Into the vehicle gas poured—a hypnotic vapor which would render the men inside unconscious. For a few moments, the rifles poked through the vents, still spitting at intervals; muffled cries sounded then, and at last, quiet.

Tim Donovan, working anxiously at Operator 5's side, turned the valve that stopped the flow of stupefying gas. He helped bring the acetylene torch again into position. Once more the blinding flame cut through the steel, rapidly marking off a huge square. The beaded margins glowed red-hot as the section sagged and dropped.

"In—quick!" Jimmy Christopher snapped. "The others are not far from their destination—this truck will be missed soon. Inside!"

Through the opening, Operator 5's men ducked. Their electric torches gleamed in the steel-walled box. On the floor, uniformed men were lying unconscious, their rifles beside them. At the wheel, the driver was sagging, asleep; his guard had fallen aside in a stupor. Against the fore-wall, small boxes were stacked, each banded with iron straps.

"Boxes used for shipping gold," Operator 5 declared tersely. "Open one—fast as you can! Before we go ahead with this plan we've got to make absolutely certain that this is what we want. When we make sure of that, the next step is the vaults! Open the nearest—now!"

OPERATOR 5 turned to a steel compartment at the front of the truck as his men tackled one of the boxes with hatchet, hammer and crowbar. The small safe had a combination dial. Operator 5 bore the acetylene torch against it. The door dropped away. Reaching in, Jimmy Christopher grasped out a heavy envelope stuffed with formidable papers.

"All the documents necessary to the freighting of this cargo!" he exclaimed.

"The box is almost open, Jimmy!" Operator 5 heard Tim Donovan exclaim.

Stuffing the documents into his pocket, he bent over the box. It was his thrust with the crowbar which tore away the last iron strap and pried up the lid. He bent, ripping aside heavy oiled paper, and peered at the metal ingot contained in the box. He stooped motionless, eyes widened, amid the sudden silence of his men.

"That's not gold!" one of them blurted.

"Not gold!"

Operator 5 rose to his feet. His implement etched a bright line on the grayish ingot of metal. He turned with haggard eyes. "Lead! Ordinary lead! Our trail of the gold stops here!"

"What?"

"Trickery! We've lost precious time!" Operator 5's voice rang bitterly. "We must abandon our entire plan!"

That tense moment flooded despair into Operator 5's heart. At this first, important step of his carefully mapped strategy, he had come to a baffling dead-end. All his hours of planning, all the risks he had run with his loyal men, had been in vain. Each danger they had chanced had become a mockery. Never before had Operator 5 felt such complete hopelessness as at this moment.

"God!" one of the men blurted in dismay. "What can we do now?"

Operator 5, listening sharply, exclaimed: "They've found the truck missing! They're coming back!"

His snapping orders sent his men ducking out of the truck. Their quick footfalls sounded in the grit. When, short minutes later, amazed guards of the caravan hurried back to the spot where a truck lay helpless, ripped open, its crew unconscious, there was no sign of the secret agents who had uncovered the amazing fakery of the ruthless international ring....

As startling was the wireless message which went crackling across the Atlantic a short time later—a message that sputtered into WDC-13 to stun Z-7:

> ... WDC-13... SPECIAL ATTENTION PRESIDENT... TACTICS ABANDONED... SHIPMENTS TO GENEVA NOT GOLD... RETURNING AT ONCE... OPERATOR 5, GSE....

IN THE President's study in the White House, four men peered at the dial of an electric clock. They were the Chief Executive, the Secretaries of State and the Treasury, and Z-7. They had been waiting long days and nights for the moment which was approaching now—the return of Operator 5.

His message, sent by wireless while he re-crossed the Atlantic, had supplied the missing details of his startling report. They knew, too, that a navy cruiser had picked him off the trans-Atlantic steamer—that at this moment he was in Washington and rushing to this historic dwelling on Pennsylvania Avenue. They waited anxiously, nervously, as the minutes twirled by....

"Operator 5 has blundered," the Secretary of State exclaimed. "He has wasted precious time on a futile effort. He's been outwitted and he has given up on the job."

"It's true," the Secretary of the Treasury agreed. "Our problem is even more serious now than before. We thought we knew where the gold was—and now we don't. We had a plan for rebuilding our finances—and now we have none. A way out of our trouble was in sight—now there is only a blank wall. It's hopeless!"

"You can wisely leave this matter in the hands of Operator 5, gentlemen," Z-7 retorted quietly.

They turned as footfalls neared in the corridor and a knock sounded at the door. The President's brisk: "Come in!" opened it. Into the study strode Operator 5, Tim Donovan at his side. The President gripped Jimmy Christopher's hand; Z-7's arm tightened affectionately across his shoulders.

"We are still absolutely at sea as to the meaning of this amazing incident, Operator 5," the President began. "What does your sudden abandonment of your mission mean?"

The ringing telephone on the President's desk checked Jimmy Christopher's response. The Chief Executive answered the summons, turned quickly: "For you, Z-7."

The chief of the Intelligence took the call. Over the wire came alarming information:

"Chief! K-3 reporting! There has been an explosion in Special

Warehouse J! The whole interior of the building has become a mass of flames. Thanks to quick action, the blaze is now under control—but it's another attack on our military stores!"

Z-7 snapped: "Watch that place—the whole section! Take every precaution to prevent a repetition of the attack!"

He lowered the phone and his eyes blazed. "A strange explosion and fire at Warehouse J! That's where we have stored our supply of ferro-manganese! It means that much of our strategic reserve has been destroyed. The sabotage ring is still working—and we are farther from being in control of the situation than ever!"

Operator 5 declared quietly: "Unless that ring is broken up, Chief, these secret attacks will continue until all our military stores are destroyed—exactly like that shipment of tin, exactly like the munitions being made at the Warwick Works. Those attacks are linked directly, you must believe now, with the international syndicate which has usurped our gold holdings."

The President asserted: "My boy, it is absolutely necessary to learn your theory about all this. Why were boxes of lead transported with such great care to vaults in Switzerland?"

"The reason?" Operator 5 smiled tightly. "A subterfuge on the part of the secret syndicate, to make us believe that the gold is out of reach—at an inaccessible spot. What does it accomplish? It places a ready weapon in the hands of the power that is planning to take control of the United States once this government is crushed out of existence!"

"What?"

THE PRESIDENT jerked to his feet. Z-7 stared, appalled.

The Secretaries of State and the Treasury peered at Operator 5 as though doubting their ears. It was the Chief Executive who asked in a whisper: "A plan to set up a new government here—you believe that?"

"No other answer is possible, gentlemen," Operator 5 declared crisply. He went on while the four men searched his face anxiously: "We know that secret forces are at work the world over. Not even this government is sure of the position of several powers which may or may not become our allies in the event of a new World War. Binding treaties have been written and signed which will determine the course of history, and the closest secrecy covers them."

"Yes—that is true!" the Secretary of State agreed.

"At the same time," Operator 5 continued, "active preparations for war have been made—more daring, on a greater scope than ever before. Of some of these we know—the plot, for instance, to establish German air bases on Irish soil for the turning of hostile craft upon England. Of others, we do not even dream. The strategy behind the false gold movements is a preparation of this sort, gentlemen, backed by the international syndicate."

The President urged tensely: "Go on!"

"We all realize," Jimmy Christopher pursued briskly, "the uneasy state of mind of the world powers. Because nations are in secret alliance and secret conflict, we cannot know which way the war will go. At best, we can only prepare to strike—sharply, quickly—once turmoil breaks out. Victory will come to the force which executes the most effective maneuver in the swiftest manner. Basically, that power will win which can soonest promise security and peace to millions of terrorized minds—and the terror of coming war, of national catastrophe, is mounting by the day!"

"You mean," the President asked tensely, "that this syndicate is preparing to take command immediately the crash comes?"

"Exactly," Operator 5 affirmed. "Picture the course events must take. First, the secret of the financial condition of this government can't be kept much longer. The facts will leak out. The result will be panic—revolution—all over the United States. Revolution is but a desperate attempt by the people to seek security. What security will they be able to find amid the collapsing of the government, the disruption of industry, the destruction of their homes? The answer, gentlemen, is that hidden gold!"

He spoke after a pause of complete silence. "Revolution breaks, out. We are without leaders. No government can exist without financial backing. Magically, that financial security appears—the gold coming from the hidden vaults of the syndicate. From it, a new national cornerstone is fashioned. It brings order out of chaos. It restores stability and peace. It gives the absolute dictatorship over the new nation to the men who control that gold—the secret syndicate."

"That is the plan!" the President exclaimed. "I am certain that must be the plan!"

OPERATOR 5 queried quietly: "Is any other possible?" There was no answer. "It explains the entire intrigue. First, the undermining of our security, the weakening of our defenses. Second, the apparent transportation of gold to divert us from the real tragedy. Third, the inevitable collapse of the United States. Fourth, a new nation built upon that same gold—controlled by European powers. Behind it all, gentlemen, everything—the success of that plan as well as the destiny of the United States—depends upon the possession of that precious store of metal."

"But—" the President asked tensely, "where is that gold?"

"I am convinced, sir," Operator 5 announced, "that it is somewhere within the boundaries of the United States."

"What?"

"That gold—still in the United States?"

"Yes," Operator 5 stated flatly. "It has been placed in a secret vault, somewhere handy, so that the syndicate which is planning the destruction of this nation may bring it into use swiftly to establish the new government."

The men in the room peered at him, startled and dismayed. They saw no uncertainty in the eyes of Operator 5. They realized now the full import of his statements. That the gold was hidden somewhere near at hand became, in their minds, an established fact. With a few words, Jimmy Christopher had banished the thought that he had failed on his vital mission. He had sounded a warning of even greater danger to the United States.

"Now, more than ever, then," the Secretary of the Treasury declared, "we must get that gold back!"

Z-7 snapped: "I'll put the entire Intelligence on the job of finding it—every man!"

"But," Operator 5 cautioned, "we must go about it swiftly and carefully. Swiftly, because once the people learn the facts and rise in rebellion, it will be too late. Carefully, because we

160

must preserve that secret as long as possible. We cannot, for instance, order out the army in a widespread search for the hidden vaults—that would betray our situation. Our search must be made in secret. It must succeed soon—for the hours in which we can possibly save ourselves are few—numbered!"

Z-7 exclaimed, "Good God! What can we do?"

"Find that gold!"

"But what lead have we to it?"

"None."

SILENCE CAME again into the President's study as the men grasped the full, appalling significance of the situation. Stunned by the revelation of the truth, appalled by the magnitude of the task forced upon them, baffled by the mystery they faced, they searched Operator 5's darkened eyes.

"Mr. President," he said quietly, "I will try my best to follow this case through to the end."

"By all means!" the Chief Executive exclaimed.

Operator 5 gripped the President's hand; he left the study quietly. He noted, as he strode along the corridor, that Z-7 was not following. Tim Donovan walked at his side and studied his dark-lined face. Near the entrance of the White House, Diane Elliot and John Christopher were waiting. They saw deep anxiety in his eyes as he forced a smile.

"I have never felt more hopeless," Operator 5 admitted quietly, "than at this moment, and yet—"

"Nonsense, Jimmy Christopher!" Diane exclaimed. "You've been right from the beginning, and you're equal to the job—I know you are. I'll never stop believing in you."

"We'll stick with you no matter what happens!" Tim Donovan averred. "To the limit!"

"Thanks, Di," Operator 5 said solemnly. "I know you will, Tim. Yet—"

The sound of a quickly opening door made Jimmy Christopher jerk around. He saw Z-7 hurrying from the President's study. The chief's face was pasty, his eyes blazing dark as he strode close and blurted: "A new attack on Warehouse J! A second explosion—a new fire! Our store of ferro-manganese is being destroyed! That building is going up in flames now!"

Operator 5 turned to the White House entrance with eyes shining. "Tim—with me! It's a chance in a million for a lead, and we've got to make the most of it! Snap into it, old-timer!"

He hurried out the entrance with the breathless lad. When he stepped into his roadster, Tim ducked. In the opposite side, Diane Elliot followed quickly. Dismayed, Operator 5 objected: "Not this time, Di!" The girl smiled, settled down, and ordered quietly: "Go ahead, Jimmy—I'm right with you!" Pressed by the urgency of the moment, he sent the car shooting out through the gate, his lips closed hard.

Spinning wheels carried him swiftly toward a spot where a power bent on destroying the nation had struck anew....

CHAPTER 11
SECRET SIGNALS

B LACK CLOUDS poured high into the sky from the flaming interior of the great warehouse. The huge brick building sat remote from the hub of the Capital, but all the fire-fighting apparatus of the city had been rushed to the scene to quench the roaring flames. Poison fumes added to the peril as the furnace consumed the vast chemical store.

Great hoses were playing streams of water upon it when Operator 5 hurried through the growing crowd to the ropes which kept the surrounding streets clear. Windows flared like dragon's eyes; walls had collapsed into black, smouldering heaps. Sparks were flying into the zenith through swelling clouds of gray and black. With difficulty, the conflagration was being brought under control, yet it was obvious that the warehouse and all it contained were doomed....

Operator 5 saw drenched, rubber-coated men rushing reports to the commander of the fire-fighting units, heard their gasping voices:

"Had it under control, but it broke right out again, Chief! Hell seemed to bust out right in the middle of it! There was an explosion and white stuff flew everywhere, eating through everything!"

The words brought a chill to Jimmy Christopher's heart. They could mean only one thing: *thermite!* Another attack by the dread, melting stuff that consumed everything it touched, that now was wasting precious military stores of the government. He listened again, and a wonder filled his mind. How, this time, had the destructive power been hurled so cunningly at its mark?

Once by air—the destruction of priceless stores of tin. Once by water—the wrecking of the great Warwick Works.

This time? It was broad daylight; the building, Operator 5

knew, had been constantly guarded so that the planting of a bomb inside it was impossible. No aircraft could have been used, no saboteur could have come close to the building, yet….

A jarring thud shocked along Operator 5's nerves. He had sensed a faint, whistling sound above the roar of the flames; and a muffled concussion ended it. The burst shook the weakened walls of the warehouse. Beyond the windows, white fire blazed blindingly. Within the doomed shell, fresh destruction struck. Into the very center of the havoc, as though to make the ruin of the precious supplies absolutely complete, a new charge of thermite had dropped at this very moment!

"There it is again!" came from one of the gasping firemen. "Same as before! God, we can't fight that! The whole thing's goin'! That wall's comin' down!"

The thunder of the collapsing wall brought a wail from the crowd as Operator 5 peered into the clouds of smoke. Was there, high in the zenith, some invisible craft hovering—dropping bombs on this mark? He doubted that at once. No craft could escape detection in daylight; and the hits were too accurate. A new thought, springing into his mind, turned him rapidly.

"After me, Tim!" he ordered. "Di, stick close!"

THEY FOUGHT their way through the mob, toward the curb where Operator 5 had parked his roadster. Once at the wheel, he sent it past the corner. In this section, the cross-streets were narrow, walled by the bleak fronts of tenements; but the radiating avenues were wide and open. He sent the roadster shuttling down one of them, then turned into another. His eyes sharpened at a truck which was drawn close to the curb in front of another warehouse, and he slowed.

"Jimmy!" Tim Donovan exclaimed. "There—that man beside the truck—the one in the overalls! He's the fellow that took me to the hideaway! He's the one named—"

"Ruffolo!" Operator 5 added in a quiet voice. "Right, Tim! We've got our lead! We're going past—keep out of sight. Di, watch that truck!"

Grimly he sent the roadster forward. The girl, glancing back, noted that the truck was headed toward the center of the city, that its rear end faced the section blackened by the fire. The high tailgate was closed, but two men were standing near it as if in readiness. Operator 5 turned the next corner quickly, then stopped the car beside a sooty building.

He strode at once to the door, found it blocked, drew out his master-keys. They opened the way into a building that once had been a small manufacturing plant. Its musty, dank air testified that it had been empty long months. Operator 5 led the way to one of the front windows.

He scanned the street, then worked the rusty catch of a window loose. Carefully, sliding it open only a few inches, he drew a small chromium mirror from his pocket. He held it beyond the sill, adjusted its angle so he could see the truck near the far corner. He noted that near the rear end, Ruffolo was still waiting, peering up and down the street.

The moment came when there was no other car in sight— when no pedestrian was on the sidewalk. Ruffolo snapped a signal. Instantly, the high tailgate of the truck leafed down.

Amazed, Operator 5 glimpsed, within the body of the vehicle, a small, carriage-mounted gun! It rolled forward. It coughed out a single, muffled report. As swiftly, it rolled back, the tailgate swung up—and it was gone from sight again.

An instant later, a dull concussion shook the ground, and a thousand voices raised a cry—a chorusing wail of the mob watching the warehouse fire.

Operator 5 drew back, his muscles tight, his eyes grim, "A small mortar hidden in that truck!" he exclaimed. "Trained on the building! It has fired charges of thermite into it! More work of the syndicate—and, thank God, a lead we can follow!"

Again he extended the mirror. Now he saw that Ruffolo and the other man had hurried to the seat of the truck. Its exhaust was sneezing out fumes as it started off. Immediately, Operator 5 signaled Tim and Diane. He hurried out of the dank building, took the wheel of the roadster, drove quickly to the next corner.

"We're following Ruffolo!"

Twice more he swung past corners; his second turn placed him behind the rattling truck. He drew to the curb and watched it until it passed from sight; then he followed again. A series of spurts carried him across the city. Presently his vigilance tightened when the truck swung into a garage. Nearby, Operator 5 stopped his roadster; his eyes narrowed.

"A flash to WDC-13, and that truck can be captured, Jimmy—the gun-crew, too!" Tim exclaimed.

"Yes, but that move would destroy our bigger chance, Tim," Operator 5 answered. "It would warn the syndicate that we're following a new lead. The truck won't be used again; the crew are only Ruffolo's subordinates. That man is our best gamble and—there he is!"

JIMMY CHRISTOPHER spoke as a car slid down the ramp of the garage. It was an expensive, powerful coupé; Ruffolo was at the wheel. Operator 5 watched him speed down the avenue; he kicked the roadster's Diesel engine into action and followed.

Now the streetlights were on, and evening was falling upon the Capital. Twilight deepened as Operator 5 followed Ruffolo's trail into another section of the city. After half an hour of circuitous driving, the espionage agent stopped his costly automobile in front of a cheap tenement in a sordid neighborhood. He waited inside it a few minutes, while Operator 5 observed him from a distance; then he turned into a garage.

Jimmy Christopher was afoot, watching from a doorway, when Ruffolo strode back and entered one of the row of dingy tenements. His keen mind had determined upon daring subterfuge. Signaling Tim and Diane to follow, he crossed the street directly toward the entrance Ruffolo had entered.

"This," he said quietly, "is probably a cover address for the syndicate—a sort of secret post office, where messages are left and picked up. Espionage agents usually appear at such places at specified times. I'm taking a chance that Ruffolo is in there alone. Stick close, both of you. If my plan works out, I'm going to need you."

Tim and Diane watched uneasily as he tried the knob of the entrance. Finding it locked, he pulled out his master-keys. He drew the bolt with the utmost quiet, opened the way without a sound, stepped into musty air. The boy and Diane followed him quietly. He advanced a few steps, paused, listening, hearing a furtive rustle of movement in one of the closed rooms beyond.

He nodded, signaled Tim and the girl to stand motionless, and approached to the door. Their eyes widened with astonishment when he deliberately rattled the knob and came back noisily. "This is the place!" he exclaimed in a voice that must surely carry to the espionage agent inside the room. "Probably it's empty, but we're taking a look around!" And he strode straight to the door of the room inside which he had heard the furtive sounds of movement.

Tim and Diane were directly behind him when he stepped in. His hand was tense for a quick draw of his automatic; but he found the room empty. Lips curved wryly, he deliberately walked to the center of the room. As he looked around, he drew a notebook and pencil from his pocket and scribbled.

Aloud he said: "Nobody here. This place is not much good to us except to watch for a possible lead."

He held the written page so Tim and the girl could see, and they read with astonishment:

Notice no dust on closet door knob—Ruffolo hiding in there—Do not let him learn we know.

"Possibly this place was used as a cover address some time ago," he said again, so that Ruffolo could hear in the closet, "but nobody's used it for a long time. There can't be anything here worth finding, but—orders are orders!"

HIS KEEN eyes searched the room as he spoke. He strode

into several adjoining rooms, then back. All of them were absolutely bare. On the floor, he noted faint tracks in the dust which led to one of the side walls. Nothing suspicious was there, except a board on which a number of old coat-hooks were screwed. Operator 5 reached to it with sharpened eyes.

"Nope—nothing here," he repeated as he pried at it. "Bum lead this time."

He choked down a cry of satisfaction as the board loosened in his fingers. It swung forward on concealed hinges, disclosing a cavity beyond. In this secret space an envelope was lying. Quickly Operator 5 took it up, noted the name *Ruffolo* scrawled on its face. Signaling extreme care to the others, he withdrew a folded sheet. His heart raced as he read:

> Report aboard Au carrier as soon as possible. Impending disruption of American government necessitates completion of plans. Final strategy for seizing government to be perfected tonight.

Operator 5's eyes burned at the phrase: "Report aboard Au carrier as soon as possible." *Au*, he knew, was the chemical symbol for gold! His mind raced as he replaced the message in its envelope, the envelope in its cavity. He pressed the leaf shut, leaving it exactly as he had found it.

Tim Donovan, carrying through Operator 5's disarming conversation for the benefit of Ruffolo in the closet, asked, "There isn't much chance of anybody's coming here, is there, Jimmy?"

Operator 5's eyes sparkled as he answered, "Not much, Tim,

but I'm ordered to watch the place. We'll stay inside for a while, I guess." He wrote in his notebook as he spoke, and passed the message to Tim, along with a key he removed from his vest pocket. The boy read:

> Go to the roadster—slip out without a sound so R will think you're still here. Use this key, open under-seat compartment and bring back black metal case.

Tim immediately began following these cryptic orders. Talking as though Tim were still present, Operator 5 took Diane's arm and led her into the next room. He placed himself so that Ruffolo could watch him through the keyhole and know that a way of escape was not yet open. In a quiet whisper which could not carry to the man's ears, Operator 5 spoke to Diane, his eyes grave.

"Di, I'm planning a risky move, and I need your help. The message I found speaks of a 'gold carrier.' That means either the gold is aboard an aircraft or a ship. The weight of the gold would rule out the first. If the gold is stored on a ship, trailing Ruffolo to it without his knowing it will be almost impossible—except in the one way I've planned."

"I'll do anything I can to help, Jimmy," the girl answered softly.

"Good! If Ruffolo realizes he is being followed, he will not go to the gold carrier—he will not betray its location. If he believes he is safe, he will follow orders and reach it. I'm positive that the trail will be so difficult, the way covered so carefully, that extraordinary means must be taken of learning its location. For that, I need your help, Di—but I warn you, it's very dangerous."

The girl declared gently: "I'm not afraid."

Operator 5's whisper continued: "Ruffolo's orders are pressing. He must get out safely at the soonest possible moment, and cover himself. He's desperate—we can count on that.

"My plan means allowing yourself to be taken away as a captive. I'm gambling that Ruffolo, because his orders are so urgent, will take you aboard the gold carrier, wherever it is."

The girl's face paled, but she answered in a hushed voice: "I'm ready!"

"Good girl!" Jimmy Christopher turned to see Tim Donovan returning. The boy came into the room quietly, carrying a small, rectangular object the size of a small book. Operator 5 moved aside from the door, took it, and explained quickly to Diane.

"This is a device I built myself. It's very simple, but right now, extremely important. It is my means of following you and Ruffolo. It is merely a buzzer arrangement supplied by a small but powerful battery. Once this release button as pushed, the buzzer acts at regular intervals—but it cannot be heard outside the case."

He took Diane's purse, opened it, placed the case inside. He touched a button, and the girl listened, but she could hear nothing.

"It's acting now," Operator 5 added. "The buzzer creates a spark. All electric sparks send out weak wireless impulses. This little transmitter is not tuned at all. Each time the sparks jump, a splash of radio impulses radiates from it—the sort of thing which is called man-made static. Similar impulses come from ordinary doorbells and electrical devices. But those impulses are going to be my means of following you and Ruffolo while you're out of sight."

"I understand, Jimmy."

"At the same time," Operator 5 continued, "messages may be sent from this device. By touching this other button, code signals may be tapped out. Again, they're not tuned—any nearby set can pick them up—and therein lies a danger. I'm going to follow you as closely as possible, and I'll pick up any message you may send—but don't change the intermittent arrangement unless you have a vital message, because it may lead to discovery."

"But what if that is taken away from me—my purse?" Diane asked quickly.

"That's another danger. You're to hold onto it as closely as possible, gambling that it will appear innocent. Don't let it out of your hands if you can possibly avoid it. All set? Tim, listen, old-timer. I'm going out of here now. I'm going to leave you and Di alone. If any attack comes, you're to pass out of the picture immediately. You're to allow Di to be kidnapped. Understand?"

Tim, eyes widened, answered, "Sure, Jimmy! But it's an awful chance!"

"It is, but we've got to take it." Operator 5 passed the purse to the girl and raised his voice so that Ruffolo, in the next room, could hear. "We'll be staying here a little while, so I'll go out to get something to eat. How about some coffee and sandwiches? I'll be right back. You won't be afraid, Di?"

"Not with Tim here with me, Jimmy," the girl answered—but her face was pale, her eyes anxious.

"Good—be right back," Operator 5 called.

His heart pounded as he walked past the place where Ruffolo was hiding. He heard Diane and Tim talking, simulating a casual conversation, when he went out. The sound of the closing entrance echoed throughout the house; Tim and Diane peered at each other anxiously a moment.

"We've got to give him the chance, Tim," the girl said in a whisper.

The boy nodded, said loudly: "Guess I'll take a look around, Di."

TIM WANDERED into the next room, then into the hallway. He crept partway up the steps and paused, looking back through the door. He saw the closet knob twist, a crack appear, and Ruffolo's eyes gleam. When Diane moved, the door closed again quickly. Suddenly the muffled purr of a bell sounded, startling the girl.

She stood motionless, realizing that the sound had come from somewhere near at hand. When it came again, she moved toward the door of a closet. Realizing that if this was a summons to a hidden telephone—that any message she might intercept would force Ruffolo to drastic measures—she deliberately searched for the instrument. She opened the door of the closet, peered into the gloom as it rang again.

The sound vibrated the boards under her feet. Stooping, she fingered at the wainscoting. Her breath caught when a section of it slid away, revealing a hollow at the floor level. She reached

173

in, lifted the instrument, pressed the receiver to her ear and whispered: "Yes?"

A hollow voice came over the wire. "Position parallel Cape Charles five," she heard—and at the same instant, quick footfalls pounded the floor in the room beyond!

She whirled and gasped. Ruffolo was rushing across the room. The girl's discovery of the telephone had lured him from his hiding place. He leaped at her with an oath as she strove to sidle out of the closet. Desperately, he gripped her arms, held her close to him, and wrenched the telephone from her hands. While she squirmed to free herself he blurted:

"Chief! The message went wrong! Ruffolo talking!"

"What?" snapped over the line. "Keep the position secret at all costs. Report as quickly as possible! Parallel Cape Charles five!"

As Ruffolo dropped the instrument, Diane tore away the fingers he had clamped over her mouth. "Tim!" she called desperately. Her heart pounded at thought of the danger confronting her, but she carried through the plan outlined by Operator 5. "Tim! Tim, help me!"

Tim Donovan had seen Ruffolo dart from the closet, but Operator 5's warning had held him back. Now, at the girl's call, he bounded down the steps. Rushing through the connecting doorway, he glimpsed Ruffolo whirling out of the closet, thrusting Diane back, shutting her inside it.

"Get away from her!" Tim shouted. Ruffolo's hand flicked to an armpit holster. The dismayed boy leaped aside as the gun glinted and spat. A bullet ripped through the side of his coat. Instantly acting out the pretense, Tim forced out a groan, sprawled on the floor. He lay motionless, breath held, apparently struck down by the bullet—but his senses were alert, his heart pounding.

He heard Ruffolo open the closet door, drag Diane out of it. He knew that the girl was struggling while Ruffolo forced her across the room. A rear entrance opened and closed. Tim deduced that Ruffolo was hurrying the helpless girl to the nearby garage by this back way. He lay motionless during an agonized moment, then sprang up. Breathlessly he rushed out the front entrance of the tenement.

His blood beat hot as he sped through the shadows to Operator 5's roadster. Jimmy Christopher was at the wheel, eyes darkened with anxiety. The boy scrambled in and blurted: "He's got her, Jimmy! He's taken her away!"

"A million to one chance, Tim—and it may cost Di's life!" Operator 5 exclaimed huskily.

He had switched on the radio. Turning the dial between two stations, he listened. Faintly from the loudspeaker a buzzing noise came. It was a faint, almost inaudible sputter until Jimmy Christopher fingered the volume control to fade out background static. *Buzz-buzz! Buzz-buzz!* Peering ahead, he saw Ruffolo's coupé shoot out of the garage, turn a corner, and pass from sight.

Buzz-buzz! Buzz-buzz!

Grimly, with the utmost caution, Operator 5 began following the trail of that faint sputtering signal—a trail leading far through a momentous night....

CHAPTER 12
VAULTS OF THE SEA

I**N THE** rumble compartment of the speeding coupé, Diane Elliot lay bound hand and foot, adhesive tape plastered across her mouth, a handkerchief tightened across her eyes. Her heart pounded with dread while she felt the car sway around corners, spurt and slow, sway again. In her one hand, she gripped the purse which contained Jimmy Christopher's invention.

Desperately she had resisted all effort to tear it from her fingers. It made no sound that she could hear. She could not tell whether it was functioning or not. Yet, in that turmoil of uncertainty, she kept hold of it and prayed that it was sending out the signal which would bring Operator 5 along the trail.

A torturous eternity passed before the car stopped. Diane felt cold air gust over her when the rumble compartment was opened. Rough hands seized her and lifted her. She could see nothing, hear nothing but quick movements and the faint lapping of water. When she was lowered, an irregular heaving told her she was on a small boat. Then a propeller churned the water and a cold wind whipped around her.

The period that followed seemed endless to the anxious girl. Her tight bonds caused an agony that grew each minute. At last, on rougher water, she felt the boat slowing. She was lifted again.

Now her hands and ankles were loosened. She was forced, still blindfolded, to grip the rungs of a rope ladder. She mounted, commanded by gruff voices, still gripping the purse containing the strange mechanism. Was it working? Was it sending out impulses which Operator 5 was following? Diane could only hope that it was marking this trail out to the open sea.

Her arms were gripped; she was forced across a deck. Its slow sway showed her that it was a large steamer. Gruff voices continued around her while she was forced down a companionway. At last she was placed in a small compartment, and the voices around her were muffled metallically. Crouched on a small seat, she felt a strange sensation—a vibration all around her, accompanied by a tightening of air pressure.

Complete silence surrounded her, save for the faint vibrating. Dulled metallic clanging sounded when it stopped. She felt a rhythmic chugging, as of pumps working, and a long period passed. Presently she was forced from the seat, pulled through a small door. That same strange soundlessness surrounded her as she was conducted along a smooth, metal floor.

When she was brought to a stop, gruff commands were spoken. Suddenly, painfully, the adhesive was stripped from her mouth. The bandage was torn from her eyes. She peered around, momentarily blinded by bright light. Then details came out of the glare, her eyes widening with amazement.

She was in what appeared to be a large, box-like room constructed completely of some metal like aluminum. In its walls were scores of doors, all closed. In front of them ran a square walk, railed on its outer side, also of metal. The center section of the great room was floored only with—water!

DIANE ELLIOT'S first impression was that this strange retreat resembled a swimming pool. The square of water in its center might be the pool itself; the small rooms beyond the

railed walk might be cabins. Yet she knew
that this was not so. The roof was of flat,
reinforced metal unbroken by any glass.
The water was strangely still. She was
oppressed by a sensation of high air pressure all around her. She saw vents above,
from which pulsing sounds emerged;
through these, air was being forced into
the room. Added to the strangeness of
the scene was the sensation of soundlessness and remoteness.

THE DIVING BELL

Ruffolo was peering at her. He took her arm, and instinctively Diane's grip on her purse tightened. Ruffolo turned her
away, opened one of the metal doors, thrust her through it. She
entered and stopped short as the door closed behind her. Turning, grasping the metal knob, she found it locked. She turned
again, to peer around the room.

The table, chair, and cot in it were all of the same silvery
metal—an extremely light and strong alloy. There was no
window—only the one locked door. This was, the girl felt, the
quarters of someone in authority in this weird place. She lowered
herself to the chair, still gripping the purse, and sat chilled with
wonder and apprehension.

A long time passed; then sharp footfalls sounded outside her
door. The knob turned; the way was opened. Diane jerked to her
feet at sight of the man who entered. He closed the door behind
him, stared at her with white eyes. He was huge, commanding in
his bearing. His face was covered with a glittering aura of light

that sparkled from the strange mask he wore—a mask fashioned of finest mesh of purest gold.

His voice was hollow, ghostly, as he said: "I bid our charming, unwilling guest welcome to our headquarters under the sea."

Diane Elliot gazed transfixed at the man in the gold mask. She pressed her lips against the words rushing to them. The white eyes of the golden-masked man glittered with a strange, mad light. Instinctively she realized that his supreme self-confidence, his utter lack of fear, might urge him to divulge information vital to Operator 5's purpose. Her chin lifted defiantly as she gazed at him.

"You wonder," his hollow voice came, "where you are? You wonder if help may come to you? I promise you that it will not. No one will ever be able to find you here—no one would dare attempt to rescue you if they knew. You are, in fact, far beneath the surface of the open sea. You are suspended between the surface above and the depths below—a prisoner in a world apart."

Diane exclaimed: "I don't believe that!"

"It is quite true," the man in the golden mask answered. "Surely you know of the age-old device known as the diving bell. It is merely a bottomless, air-tight box. When lowered beneath the surface, the air pressure within it keeps the water out and observations may be made. You have only to push an ordinary drinking glass beneath the surface of a pail of water, upside-down, to see the effect. You are in a large, elaborate, scientifically planned diving bell which was constructed for a very special purpose."

Now the strangeness of her surroundings was fully explained to the girl, but still she simulated disbelief.

"This huge bell," the man in the golden mask continued, "is automatically stabilized by special devices. It remains always on an even keel. Perhaps you think it is supported under the surface by chains connecting with ships above? Not at all. Only one thing holds it poised in its present position—air pressure. From a single ship on the surface, air-lines lead down. The pressure is maintained to a fraction of a pound. Added or lessened weight is automatically and instantly taken care of. Literally you are suspended in the sea by a most delicate balance.

"If the men in charge of the pumping station above should choose, they could send this bell down at an instant's notice—kill everyone aboard—drop this device far to the bottom of the ocean. It is quite deep here. We are five miles off Cape Charles. Should this bell sink, it would be far beyond the reach of the bravest diver—far beyond any possible reclamation—with the nation's vast store of gold aboard it!"

DIANE ELLIOT'S heart sped. "You are astonished?" the man in the golden mask asked. "It is true, I assure you. The most precious store of gold in the world is aboard—gold absolutely vital to the existence of the United States—hanging precariously in the balance. You understand now why I say you cannot be rescued? Even if the location of this bell be discovered, even if agents of the United States Government succeed in reaching it—it would be futile. One touch of a valve will send the gold plunging to the bottom of the sea!

"Even this is not all. We have planned even against the possibility that the pumps might be seized and the valve kept shut by an attacking party. In a space, low in the hull of the ship above us, there is a special crew. It might be called the Destroying Watch. Those men are kept constantly on the alert. Never is that watch allowed to lapse for a moment. If the valves should be seized, those men are prepared to send the ship to the bottom—in a way that cannot possibly be stopped—and it will carry this bell with it even with the valves still closed!"

Consternation lighted the girl's eyes while she listened.

"You were brought here because of the information you possess concerning this craft's location. You will never reveal that information. Even if you could, it would not help to return the gold to the United States. I am prepared to drop that treasure to the bed of the ocean rather than see it returned to Washington!

"Now you know! The United States faces certain destruction! In a few hours, panic will sweep across the country! Nothing can save the nation but this gold—and we control it! If any attempt is made to wrest it from us, it will plunge into the sea, lost forever! Destruction—do you hear? I have promised destruction to the nation which destroyed me, and now that promise will be fulfilled!"

While Diane stared, the man in the golden mask turned quickly. He snapped open the door, stepped out, slapped it shut. The bolt clicked into its socket. Dismayed, chilled, Diane tried to open it, found the way stoutly barred. She retreated, overcome with a sense of hopelessness.

In her trembling hands she still held the purse containing the Hertzian wave device. Now she brought it out. She pressed the second of the two buttons. Quickly, realizing the danger of the attempt, she tapped that button in Morse code and telegraphic shorthand:

Gold carrier suspended beneath surface five miles off Cape Charles on parallel. Air pressure balances it in place, supplied pumping station steamer above. On attack, pressure will be destroyed and bell will plunge, carrying gold with it.

While footfalls sounded again outside her door, Diane hurried, continued to tap her message out in code. With desperate quickness, she returned the device to her bag as the door snapped open. Ruffolo strode in, his face suffused with anger. He stared at her, blurted:

"Our radio receiver is picking up signals! Some kind of a message about this bell! Do you know anything about that?"

Diane stared in consternation. Ruffolo straightened, muttering, "How the devil could you be sending radio signals, anyway?" He peered around, then strode quickly to the girl. His fingers probed into the pockets of her suit, emptied them. He snatched her purse out of her hands. A gasp of dismay broke from the girl's lips.

Angrily Ruffolo whirled. The purse containing the Hertzian device splashed into the strangely still water beyond the rail, disappeared in the dark depths of the sea…!

THICK NIGHT spread over the ocean beyond Cape Charles. No stars gleamed through the bank of fog floating high. There was no glimmer in all that expanse of darkness save the shining decks and ports of a coastwise vessel ploughing north farther out from the shore. Fog enveloped it, blanketed it away; the blackness became unbroken. Yet, in the dark depths, there was a winged presence....

High in the sky, a weird craft hovered. The vanes of an auto-gyro whirred gently in the sea wind. A propeller slashed the air and an engine purred through a muffled exhaust. In the pit of the poised gyro, two figures huddled. One bent to the controls—Tim Donovan. The other, Operator 5, hunched low over the radio installation of the craft.

The strange trail of the buzzing signals had taken Jimmy Christopher into the black zenith. Following the faint sound through the streets of Washington, he had been led to the bank of the Potomac north of the city. Becoming certain that Ruffolo had carried Diane away by water, he had hastily ordered this gyro—a special craft of the army—made ready at Bolling Field. Tim Donovan had manipulated the controls while he swung out across the bay, striving to follow the intermittent buzzing that meant he was still close to Ruffolo and the girl.

He had heard the signals become fainter and fainter. He had heard them cease, then come again in the form of dots and dashes. He had scribbled the message swiftly while amazement grew in him. There had come a break in the impulses, and Operator 5's heart stopped with them. Now, abruptly, they broke off again.

"Jimmy!" Tim Donovan exclaimed, thumping his shoulder. "Look directly below! A boat without lights!"

Operator 5 raised cautiously. Tim Donovan had sent the muffled gyro hovering low in an attempt to reach a position in which the buzzing signals might be heard more strongly. His keen eyes had discerned vague outlines on the water. Jimmy Christopher, peering over the cowling, saw the faint dim shape.

"Yes—a steamer! Its ports all covered, its decks dark! It's the boat Diane mentions—"

He peered at the message he had scrawled, and as he re-read the last words, his heart grew cold:

> Gold-masked man aboard. Declares any attempt to take gold means sending it to bottom. Turn of valve will send it plunging. Valve may be on steamer—may be here. Any attempt to seize gold seems hopeless, but—

There the message had ended.

"Jimmy!" Tim Donovan exclaimed as he peered at the words in the dim glow of the dash. "What can we do?"

"Regardless of the danger, Tim, we've got to get that gold back into the Treasury!" Operator 5 declared grimly.

"But—but if that threat is carried out, Jimmy, and the gold is sent to the bottom, Diane—"

"I know, Tim," Jimmy Christopher answered, his voice grave. "She'll—" He broke off savagely. "She'd want me to go ahead—to make the try—and I'm going to!"

Quickly, Operator 5 trimmed the oscillator of the radio transmitter to reach the Washington Intelligence headquarters, and snapped a distorter into the circuit. His voice rang imperatively out over the ether: "Calling WDC-13! Operator 5 calling WDC-13 and Z-7! Urgent! Urgent!"

THROUGH THE air, an answer crackled: "WDC-13 picking you up! Z-7 coming to the mike! Stand by!" A moment later the voice of the Washington chief followed: "Z-7 speaking! What's your report, Operator 5?"

"The vault containing the hidden gold has been located, Chief! Hidden beneath the surface of the sea, making it almost impossible to reach. But we've got to make the try! I have instructions—"

"What?" Z-7 broke in. "How the devil can we—?"

"There's no time for explanations now, Chief!" Operator 5 interrupted. "It's a desperate chance we must take. Please follow these instructions as quickly as possible. Order all available men into boats—the fastest you can find. All boats bring hook-ropes. Proceed carefully to a point five miles off Cape Charles. All lights out! Watch for a signal from the air to stand by. I'll come down and organize the attack. You must bring deep-sea diving suits—all you can get! Long lines and the necessary air pumps. The boats carrying this apparatus are to stand off until given a signal to advance. Avoid a steamer without lights, riding at the point I've mentioned. It must not know we are approaching. That's vital, Chief—otherwise the store of gold will be lost!"

"Coming! As soon as possible!"

"Watch for my signal and I'll descend to your boat, Chief!"

Quickly Jimmy Christopher again trimmed the oscillator. This time he snapped the distorter out of the circuit. Realizing that his new call was a grave risk, he hesitated; but again he spoke ringingly:

"Calling X! Calling X!"

Out of the ether came a voice: "X reporting!" It was spoken in the tones of X-13—John Christopher.

"Marshal the Hidden Hundred!" Jimmy Christopher commanded. "Send men by boat to a point five miles off Cape Charles! Order them to prepare to board a steamer at a triple red signal! Warn them that Intelligence men are entering into this case—that it may mean certain capture for some of them—but we need their help! There is no time to lose! Get the Hidden Hundred into action at once!"

"Orders will be followed!"

Operator 5 signaled Tim Donovan, and the gyro soared high. Again Jimmy Christopher attempted to pick up the faint buzzing signal that Diane Elliot had sent. Vainly he tried—it was gone…. When he was certain that no further message would come from the depths of the sea, Operator 5 sat tense in the pit, searching the blackly heaving sea through powerful binoculars, waiting….

UNSEEN IN the night, their courses unmarked by even the faintest glimmer, boats came flocking to sea. Thick darkness covered their movements as their screws churned the water at top speed. They were craft brought into action by the swift orders of Z-7, carrying Intelligence men. Coast-guard cutters, power launches, every manner of craft that could be found swarming over the face of the ocean, following secret orders.

Z-7 stood on a dark, windy deck, with trusted agents around him. They had commandeered a small coastwise steamer then at anchor in the bay. It was plunging through the swells as fast as the screws could churn.

But that craft was slower than the smaller, more powerful boats carrying still other agents eastward. In the dark, they sped past Z-7. Then, when the chief's calculations showed that he was nearing the objective, they slowed and rode the swells in response to his flashing signal.

Unknown to Z-7 and the Intelligence men, still additional craft were plunging through the waves. The men aboard them were backed by no official power. Theirs was the loyalty to their captain's orders. Fast cars had carried them to the waterfront; they had seized forcibly such boats as they could find. As they drove away from shore in their lightless craft, in supreme command, they made up a weird company. They were wearing the skull masks and the skeleton gloves of the Hidden Hundred...!

On the flagship of his hastily ordered fleet, Z-7 braced himself against the wind and peered through strong binoculars into the sky. He swung his glasses across the zenith; his motions froze when he caught a glimmer of light. High in the air, an electric torch was blinking. Immediately the chief snapped commands. A searchlight, its lens hastily black-taped so that only a sparkle of light was emitted—hooded so that its light could be seen from only one direction—blinked upward.

A fluttering sound came out of the sky in response to an answering signal. In the darkness, a weird craft hovered. Z-7 crossed the deck rapidly as he glimpsed the spinning vanes of the descending gyro. It swooped low over the deck, became motionless, floated downward. Its fat tires bounced and its muffled

From the lips of an officer the command rang: "Open the valves!"

engine whispered off. Operator 5 climbed rapidly out of the pit with Tim Donovan.

"Chief!" Jimmy Christopher strode close to Z-7. "Are all preparations made? Is the diving equipment broken out?"

"We're ready, Operator 5. But Great Scott—what does this move mean?"

Rapidly Operator 5 outlined the information relayed to him by Diane Elliot. "She's a prisoner in that great bell now, Chief! The gold is down there with her. She's warned us that the mere turning of a valve, either on the steamer or aboard the bell, may send it plunging with the gold to the bottom. We must act with the utmost caution. Otherwise, the nation is doomed. Our failure will cost not only the gold, but—Diane's life."

Z-7 asked huskily: "Your orders?"

"Chief," Operator 5 said quietly, "I have considered every possibility. My first thought was to send divers down to find the bell—to attach cables to it so that it could not be sent to the bottom. I discarded that plan for several reasons. First, the hunt underwater for the bell would consume too much time; we might be discovered in the process. Second, the syndicate has surely taken a precaution against that possibility, because it is the first suggestion for attack that would naturally come to mind. I doubt that there are any means of attaching cables to the bell. Because time is so pressing, I abandoned that thought in favor of a plan offering us far better chances."

JIMMY CHRISTOPHER pointed across the water. "There, in that direction, though you can't see it, Chief, lies the steamer carrying the pumps which keep the bell suspended.

Men are on duty at the controls constantly—that's sure. We must take them absolutely by surprise. Remember there are two units—the ship and the bell—and if one succeeds in communicating with the other, our move will fail. We must manage to board that boat and take command swiftly. Then we must plan to take command of the bell separately."

"In God's name, how can we do that?" Z-7 demanded, staring, appalled at Operator 5.

"First, signal all our men on the other boats to approach the steamer with the greatest care. They must not be seen. We must get aboard. Absolutely nothing must stop us from taking control. Order the boats carrying the diving equipment to hang back, and all the suits brought into use except one—for me. Depending upon the success of our first move, we'll use those suits to reach the bell."

"By all means, supervise sending those orders so that we make no error. One slip now will be fatal!" Z-7 exclaimed.

Operator 5 climbed to the bridge of the steamer. There, with a flashlight taped to cut off most of its beam, and equipped with a directional hood, he flashed gleaming signals into the night. He could not see the boats he was attempting to reach, but once he completed his orders and flashed "Repeat back!" faint twinkles appeared across the swells.

Dim flashes, dot-dashing out of the night, invisible to anyone aboard the mysterious steamer, verified the receipt of the commands by the Intelligence men on the lurking boats. He raised his torch again and, grim-eyed, peered into the gloom of the sea. Farther beyond, unknown to the Intelligence men, other boats were riding the swells—the craft of the Hidden Hundred.

His lens beaconed swiftly: "Proceed upon orders!"

Out of the night the answers flashed: "Proceeding upon orders! Approaching steamer!"

While the engines of Z-7's craft churned slowly, Operator 5 drew Tim Donovan aside. The boy was wide-eyed, anxious; he searched Jimmy Christopher's face in bewilderment. He followed to the side of the gyro, and from its pit, Operator 5 removed a Very pistol. He placed it in Tim's hand, stuffed reserve charges into the boy's pockets.

"Tim, this is important! With this gun you must signal the Hidden Hundred. Three red flashes will bring them into action. It will be necessary the moment we board the syndicate steamer. There aren't enough Intelligence men to handle the situation safely—we need the Hidden Hundred, and it will be up to you to signal them so that Z-7 won't know."

"I'll handle it, Jimmy!"

"Good boy! Watch sharp! Remember—the moment we're aboard and in command!"

Z-7's craft was shoving quietly across the swells. From scattered points, Operator 5 knew, boats carrying the other Intelligence men were also approaching the lightless steamer belonging to the espionage ring. Somewhere farther back in the gloom were still others, waiting further orders—the boats carrying the diving apparatus. At the rail, Jimmy Christopher peered, searching for the outlines of the secret ship.

They appeared vaguely out of the night. Immediately Operator 5 spoke a signal. The churning screws reversed. Men rushed to the davits of the lifeboats. Turning oiled gears swung the boats over the rail. Intelligence men clambered into them carrying coils of rope. Once they were riding the swells, oars cut into the water noiselessly to carry them close to the syndicate ship. OUT OF the darkness around the boat, other craft appeared silently. Operator 5's whispered directions brought his own boat close to the hull. He glanced, saw Tim Donovan nearby. The boy was concealing the Very pistol beneath his coat. Operator 5 uncoiled a hook-rope, poised it, hurled it. It whipped upward, fell. He tried again, and the strand whipped across the rail. He pulled it, and the hook caught.

All around the ship, he knew, other men were performing the same task. The faint clinking of the rubber-covered hooks might, he knew, raise an alarm. The possibility made quick action vital. Operator 5 gripped the rope and pulled himself up rapidly. By the time he was reaching for the rail, another man was climbing behind him. He darted across the deck, huddled in the shadow of a ventilator, waited while two more Intelligence men crouched beside him.

Tense minutes passed. During that interval, Operator 5 knew, the Intelligence men were swarming over the rail from all points. The steamer's decks were deserted, black. The secret maneuver had reached a vital point without a betraying alarm. Now Operator 5's lips puckered, and he whistled a low signal. Immediately, from their hiding places on the deck, the Intelligence men sprang into action.

Trained in surprise tactics, they scattered to vital points. Some darted to the companionway to the bridge. Others hurried to the officers' quarters. Operator 5 led a wary detachment below deck. As he darted down the companionway, he heard a breathy pulsing in the air, and knew that the sound was beating from the valves of the air-compression pumps. Quick, noiseless steps carried him to a closed door. There, his signal stopped his men.

Guns in hand, they poised for a rush. What lay behind that door none of them could know. As they waited during a tense minute, Tim Donovan watched them, his one hand gripping the butt of the Very gun. The wheezing, pumping sound continued. Operator 5, tensely, in scarcely a whisper, uttered a command: "In!"

He thrust the door wide and rushed. His men raced in behind him. They burst into a brightly lighted space in which gigantic machinery was working. Around the huge drums and pistons of the air pumps, men and officers were on duty. Several in uniform were standing in front of great panels of gauges, watching the flickering needles of pressure indicators. At the opening of the door, at the first rush of Operator 5's Intelligence men, an alarm shot through the air.

From the lips of an officer near the indicator panels a command rang out: "Open the valve!"

The cracking report of Operator 5's gun broke into the words. A bullet burned across the man's face. The slug spattered, cracked the shining black surface as a grimy hand raised to the huge handle of the valve. A second shot rocked across the room; and that man recoiled in abject terror. Jimmy Christopher leaped past him, gun glittering, whirling to block the way to the handle.

"Back—and stay back!" he commanded.

His gun cracked again—at another man who was leaping toward a wall telephone. The bullet clanged against steel and scattered into countless stinging bits. Blinded, the officer recoiled. Instantly Z-7 leaped, brushed him aside, seized the contact of the telephone and held it down. Throughout the room, Intelligence men were rushing, guns glittering, covering the pump crew.

IN THE doorway Tim Donovan stood an instant, eyes widened, anxious. He whirled unnoticed, raced up the companionway. He bounded aft, to the rail. Three times he thrust charges into the Very pistol; three times, rapidly, he shot the red flares into the air. Those racking red comets would signal the Hidden Hundred into action. As the third charge streaked off into the blackness of the night, he whipped back.

He ducked low into the shadow of a ventilator as an Intelligence man shouted: "Somebody fired a signal! Find the man who fired that signal!"

Tim Donovan huddled low while heels pounded the deck—while Intelligence men rushed into a hunt which, if successful, would brand him as being in league with the Hidden Hundred!

Below deck, in the huge pump-room, a hush had fallen. The Intelligence men were in command. Their weapons were forcing the officers and the crew of the syndicate steamer from their posts. Helplessly, the members of the espionage ring faced the Intelligence men as Operator 5's voice rang commands:

"Z-7! Watch that telephone! Let no man use it! It connects with the bell, and if an alarm is sounded below it will mean failure! R-4! Take command of this gauge-board!"

A grim-faced Intelligence man stepped forward. "Yes, sir!"

"Watch those dials! Try these valves very carefully, very slowly, and learn exactly how they function! Once you're sure of what you're doing, keep those pressures exactly! That's the most important job you've ever tackled. All other men! Keep those pumps working!"

Now quick footfalls sounded at the entrance of the room. An Intelligence man rushed in, stopped short, stared aghast at Z-7. He blurted an alarm that whitened the chief's face and brought a surge of relief to Operator 5's heart:

"The Hidden Hundred! They're boarding the ship!"

CHAPTER 13
DIVE TO DOOM

JIMMY CHRISTOPHER'S voice rang into the astonishment that showed on the face of every Intelligence man.

"Chief! We can't leave our stations! If we attempt to take any of the Hidden Hundred now, it will be at the cost of our object! In this crisis, we've got to allow them to cooperate with us! We need their help!"

Z-7 stood motionless with wrath and dismay. On the companionway, heels were beating. Now strange figures moved

195

into the light. They were living skeletons—men whose heads were covered by skull masks, whose claw hands were gripping automatics. They strode fearlessly into the great pump-room while Z-7 glared at them in impotent rage.

The leader of the squad of skeletons—X-13, John Christopher—faced the chief grimly. "With your permission, Z-7, we will help you keep control of this ship!"

Operator 5 urged: "Let them, Chief! There's no other way! We dare not take a chance until we've seized the bell. That's the next step, and it must be taken immediately."

He hurried from the room, ran onto the deck. At the rail he brought out his torch and clicked out a code message. Across the swells, orders flashed to those waiting ships which carried the diving equipment. "Draw close!" Then he stepped back, waiting, while screws churned black water.

Cold anxiety filled Jimmy Christopher. The swift surprise attack had brought the syndicate steamer under control, but that success would mean nothing unless it could be repeated aboard the great bell hidden below the surface. Diane's message flashed through his mind. A single alarm would send the precious store of gold plunging to the bottom of the ocean—and with it all hope of saving the nation from chaos!

He peered around, saw that Intelligence men and members of the Hidden Hundred were stationed together on the deck. He snapped orders to the official undercover agents that no captures were to be made as long as his strategy was incomplete. Tim Donovan came to his side, anxious-eyed, breathless. The boats carrying the diving equipment loomed out of the night; and Operator 5 hurried to one of the dangling ropes.

He pendulumed to the deck; Tim Donovan slipped down after him. He paused, peering at a grotesque sight. Following his orders, three Intelligence men had already donned the bulky undersea outfits. Their bodies were completely encased in the mammoth suits. Their helmets were ready; men were at the pump-handles, ready to go into action. Others were waiting at the rail. Again Operator 5 gave commands.

"Keep this position! Make ready to dive! We'll go down together. Use your underwater torches for signaling when you sight the bell!"

While Tim Donovan watched anxiously, Operator 5 began to get into the diving suit. He pulled it over his body; the wrist-bands were strapped tight; the collar was studded in place; great leaden soles were fastened on the shoes. Meanwhile, the helmets of the others were being twisted tight. Operator 5's was adjusted and he stood ready, while the airlines writhed and the pumps began to work.

With the others, he mounted a grilled platform. A winch chugged and the platform rose on a cable. It swung out over the rail, down. Tim Donovan watched as the four men gripped the braces, as the stage lowered to the surface. Operator 5 gave a signal; it dropped again. The inky blackness of the water welled up over the bodies of the four. Their globular heads vanished beneath the surface and white bubbles popped on the surface....

BENEATH THE surface of the sea, the platform stopped, swinging slightly, suspended. Operator 5 peered about in the complete darkness. He touched the button of his torch, and a gleam shot through the blue-green water. The lamps of the other men reached out similar shafts of faint light. The radiance disappeared only a few yards away; the four were surrounded by black walls of water beyond which it was impossible to see. Operator 5 spoke crisply into the telephone mouthpiece inside his helmet.

"Down!"

One of the men on the deck above answered:

"You must wait until your body becomes accustomed to the pressure. The same way coming up, except that it's much slower then. Otherwise you'll get the bends—horrible pain—maybe death. If you—"

"Down!" Operator 5 commanded hoarsely. "We can't wait. We've got to take the chance. If the bell is directly below us, it can't be far. There's no reason for its being very deep below the surface. Let us down on the ropes! We're going off the platform."

"As you say, sir!"

Operator 5 signaled the three other grotesque figures. They felt their ropes tighten. Operator 5 was the first to step off the platform—into black, ominous space. The others followed him. Immediately, the stage swung from them, disappeared upward. They were left dangling in the water, like four helpless marionettes, with the water pressing a threat of death against them.

Jimmy Christopher scarcely felt that as he was being lowered. The sameness of the water around him was baffling. By the sense of increased pressure alone did he know that he was sinking deeper. It increased steadily, creeping upward from the legs, mounting to the chest and making breathing difficult. Again he signaled the men dangling near him, adjusted the intake and exhaust valves so that the increased pressure of the air inside his suit counteracted the crushing force of the water.

"Sir!" An alarmed tone from above rang into his ears. "I beg you not go—"

"Down!" Operator 5 growled grimly.

He knew well the danger he was facing. The increased pressure of air in his body was dissolving nitrogen in his blood. A too speedy descent might render him unconscious. A fast ascent, likewise, threatened death—torturous pain at least. Upon rising, the decreased pressure allowed the dissolved nitrogen to pass out of the blood. Accumulating in the capillaries, clogging the flow of the blood, it caused exquisite agony and sometimes death. Yet Operator 5 snapped the urgent command:

"Down!"

DANGER BENEATH the surface! They must face it now in multiple forms. Only the air pressure within their suits saved these four from being crushed by the steadily increasing weight of the water. It was an inexorable, merciless force. If, through some accident, the air pressure within the suits should suddenly lessen, all the terrific weight of the water would bear down upon them. Operator 5 had seen divers who had suffered this fate—their bodies crushed to jelly, mashed into their helmets—as horrible a death as a man might suffer.

Deeper they went, lowered steadily, while the gleam of their lamps was the only world they knew—a world that descended with them. Abruptly, Jimmy Christopher, peering past his dangling, leaded feet into the gleam of his torch, commanded: "Slower!"

He saw something shining in the light. In the glow, a school of small fish swam, then darted away—but it was something below them that attracted Operator 5's attention. A smooth surface! He gripped the rope so that he would not strike it with his leaden shoes, called into the telephone transmitter:

"Warn the other men that they must make no sound when walking on the bell!"

He hung suspended while the message was relayed to the three others in the diving outfits; then he lowered himself with the utmost care. The three drifted down beside him. In amazement, they peered through the glass of their helmets at the smooth metal surface on which they were standing. It was, they knew, the roof of the huge diving bell which contained the precious store of gold—gold on which the destiny of the United States depended.

"Operator 5!" a voice from above announced. "A report from aboard the steamer! R-4 wishes to inform you that he has the valves under control and is maintaining pressure. He has learned how to increase the pressure in the great bell, if necessary. By driving more air into it, it can be made to rise!"

Jimmy Christopher answered swiftly: "Order R-4 to stand by! He dare not attempt to lift the bell yet. There certainly are gauges inside it which will betray its movement. R-4 must wait for my signal—then lift the bell as rapidly as possible. We are on top of it now!"

"Yes, sir!"

Operator 5 again relayed orders to the three men at his side. His words had to be carried up to the deck and down again on the telephone wires: "Move in four directions! Find the edge. Lower yourselves and try to enter from below! That's the only way!"

Again information came from above. "Orders relayed! Further report from the ship! It is equipped with a smaller diving bell for communicating with the larger one now below the surface! The machinery is under control and its use is understood. It is also a means of escape from the big bell. Shall we make use of it, sir, to send men below?"

"By no means!" Operator 5 answered. "There must be no premature alarm! Everything depends on it! Wait for my signal to raise the big bell. If, by any chance, signals come up for the use of the smaller one, obey them!"

"Standing by, sir!"

Operator 5 gestured to the three other grotesque figures who stood in that black underwater world. They began moving away. Each swing of arm and leg was made with torturous slowness, not only due to the drag of the water, but because they were taking every caution against clanging their leaden shoes against the metal plates. They could not cast off these weights; for if they did so, they would shoot to the surface like bubbles, helpless, doomed to torture by the bends, perhaps to die with the bursting of their suits. Upon those leaden shoes their lives depended now—and yet they were a constant danger, a possible source of alarm.

WITH AGONIZING slowness Operator 5 walked. His

three undersea companions were lost from sight now. His torch gleamed dimly ahead of him. His head felt light and he fought to keep it clear against the effects of the too-rapid increase in pressure. Bubbles poured from his helmet as he came to a pause, peering through the faceplate of his helmet. Fish whisked past while he made sure that the surface on which he was walking ended abruptly directly in front of him.

He shifted, and his heart pounded when he found a hand-grab near the edge. Peering overside, into deep black, down the wall of the great bell, he saw the others. Ordering his men to look for similar ladders—placed there, Operator 5 knew, during the construction of the bell, and as an aid to repairs should it be brought to the surface—he gripped the highest. He breathed, "Going lower!" into the telephone transmitter—and slowly descended.

When he paused it was because the wall ended at his weighted feet. The profound gloom of the sea lay beneath him. Gingerly he gripped the rungs tightly, and stepped off into the water. Now dangling, he lowered himself by his hands until his head was level with the lower edge of the wall. He turned his light, and saw that the handholds continued on the underside. Quickly he relayed his information over the wire, and began pulling himself under the monster device.

"All three men report themselves down the walls and moving under, sir!"

Operator 5 fastened his light to a hook on his belt as he went farther beneath the shell. He half-floated as he shifted from rung to rung. Now the safety-rope was useless to him for support. It could save him from a plunge into the depths if his hands slipped, but it could not aid him toward his objective. In front of him, as he moved, he saw a glow appear and brighten. He moved into the green-blue shine; and above him he found the last of the handholds at another metal edge.

Carefully he raised himself, reaching up. He felt his hand pass out of water, into air. Heart pounding, he groped, and his fingers gripped a metal rail. Again he raised himself. His helmet lifted above the surface of the water and he peered around at a strange sight—a square space, railed with metal, surrounded by a catwalk, flanked by metal walls in which there were rows of doors. And while he looked, he saw another head appear in the square of water. Then three helmets poised, shining above the surface. He raised an arm to signal: "Up!"

Ponderously, the four men rose from the water, pulled themselves over with air-lines trailing after them. They stood on the metal walk, still breathing air pumped to them from the surface. There was no sound in their ears save the beating of the valves. There was no one in sight save their own grotesque figures. Through the telephone system, Operator 5 sent a jubilant report: *"Aboard!"*

CHAPTER 14
CONFESSED DEFEAT

A GAIN OPERATOR 5 spoke into the transmitter— orders to be relayed to his three companions on the walk: "Remove your suits!"

Stepping carefully, their air-lines trailing after them, they moved together. Standing at one side of the enclosed space, while the black water rippled, they detached their leaden soles and belts. Jimmy Christopher twisted the helmet of the nearest; each loosened the screw-joints of the others. Unfastening the collar bolts, they stripped out of the bulky suits. Alertly, breathing tightly, they peered around.

The interior of the shell seemed to be a dead thing. There was no sound save a heavy panting from the valves opening through the metal ceiling. A faint, inaudible vibration was sensible in the metal walk, a sign that machinery was working—the devices which kept the great bell constantly stabilized. All the doors were closed. Signaling his men to remain beside him, Operator 5 passed quietly along the rail.

On some of the doors, metal plates were affixed. *Stabilizer Control,* read one. Another: *Elevator.* This, Jimmy Christopher knew, must contain the receiving stage of the bell device by which passengers were lowered and raised between this undersea craft and the steamer above. He looked in, saw great circular valve-handles on the walls, many indicators, and another door which, the packing in its frame revealed, was sealed against the outside water pressure. He passed on and read other plates: *Generators; Radio Room;* and then a long series labeled: *Vault.*

He found these doors locked. Each was equipped with a combination dial. Here, in these undersea strongrooms, the gold belonging to the United States Treasury was stored! On each side of the black pool was a series of them. Behind these doors lay ingots of precious metal which might yet go plunging down into the depths of the ocean!

Operator 5 passed two doors labeled: *Quarters.* He was passing a third when he was startled by a knock on the inside. Standing stock still, motionless, he heard a voice call through—and the sound of it set his heart to racing.

"Won't you let me out? Why must you keep me a prisoner in here?"

Diane! Operator 5's hand shot to the bolt. He withdrew it quickly, thrust the way open. The startled girl recoiled and stood stock still, peering at Jimmy Christopher. His name rushed to her lips in a glad cry; but instantly, aware of the danger, she choked it back. She rushed from the room, flung her arms around Operator 5, and sobbed silently while she clung to him.

"Steady, Di!" Jimmy Christopher cautioned. "Good work— but we've only begun!"

"Jimmy! Be careful!" the girl whispered. "I heard the man in the golden mask talking to Ruffolo outside this door after I sent my message! I couldn't let you know then, but what I was afraid of is true. There's a valve down here that will open the bulkheads and release all the air! There's an engineer on duty at it constantly."

Operator 5's eyes sharpened. "Stick with me, Di," he cautioned, and he signaled his three men to follow. He passed from door to door, paused at one lettered: *Conference.* Behind it, there was muttering of voices. Operator 5 did not pause to listen. He glided on, stopped again with his gaze sharpened upon another identifying plate: *Valve Room.*

OPERATOR 5 drew back and whispered to the three operators: "This is the most vital point aboard the bell. If those valves are released, we will lose everything. Watch this door. In case of an emergency, think only of saving this craft. Take control of the stabilizing machinery and the bell-elevator. We must make the move swiftly—but wait!"

Jimmy Christopher gestured his men and Diane to stand there while he glided back to the door of the conference room. Now the voices inside were speaking distinctly. A commanding tone silenced them—the hollow, ghostly voice of the man in the golden mask. Operator 5 listened intently.

"Patience! It is only a matter of hours until the truth will be revealed to the people of the United States—until the revolution, the panic begins! We are ready to act in a moment's notice. We shall take control of the crumbling government and strengthen it anew—make it our own! Our plan is almost complete—and you, gentlemen, shall become the rulers of the new nation!"

Another mutter was silenced by the man in the golden mask. "You—the greatest industrialists of Europe! Your syndicate will become the United States of America—your word will be the new law! Your names—famous now on the continent as the powers guiding great armament works, the great ammunition factories, the great airplane plants—will become world-renowned as the kings of America! You ask me, gentlemen, if I will be content with my share—"

Now a silence pervaded, broken at last by the hushed, hollow tones of the man in the golden mask:

"Here and now, gentlemen, I return my promised share to you. I wish none of your power. I wish none of your loot. I want no part in the rule of the new nation. I am rewarded with the destruction of the existing United States. My purpose will be accomplished within a few hours. I swore, almost two decades ago, that I would destroy this nation as it destroyed me, and I have succeeded! That gentlemen, is a reward richer to me than all the power in the world!"

There followed, ringing in Operator 5's ears, a burst of hollow, mocking laughter of a man who was mad....

Operator 5 drew back swiftly as heavy footfalls sounded within the room. Suddenly, dismaying him with its swiftness, the metal door flashed open. Upon the sill, the man in the golden mask paused, startled.

Behind him, as he stood motionless an instant, Jimmy Christopher glimpsed faces that chilled him—features he recognized as those of European industrialists whose power controlled entire governments! Revealed to him were the leading minds of the syndicate formed to sack the United States. But more appalling than this were the white eyes of the gold-masked man, blazing now with mad anger.

The hollow, commanding voice boomed out: *"Open the valves!"*

Operator 5 whirled on. He sped along the metal walk toward the door of the valve-room. He saw it flash open, saw an engineer in black uniform appear. Behind this man, he glimpsed huge panels studded with pressure indicators—and a great handle. The shining metal valve-release was enclosed in a glass case. A hammer was hanging beside it. Again, as Jimmy Christopher dashed toward the opened door, the order rang out in the ghostly, imperative tone of the man in the golden mask:

"Open the valves!"

THE ENGINEER leaped back, thrusting at the door. Operator 5 flung himself into the closing crack. His arm pushed through, and the biting edges of metal shot excruciating pain through his body as they knifed together. He shouldered against it with all his power, thrust it wide. As he leaped in, he saw the hammer swing against the glass case, saw fragments glitter as they flew.

The engineer's hand gripped the handle of the valve. Operator 5's automatic spat. His bullet shattered bone as it drove into the outstretched arm of the engineer. A howl of rage and pain broke from the uniformed man's lips as he staggered away. Jimmy Christopher whirled, conscious of shouts on the walk, heels hammering the metal plates. Guns blasted hollowly, echoing explosions within the huge, steel-walled room. He whirled, backed to the valve. His second bullet spattered against the wall and sent the terrorized engineer rushing out.

Straddled, eyes narrowed, gun leveled, he blocked the way to the handle—one throw of which would decide the fate of a nation.

Again shots blasted beyond the door. Operator 5 glimpsed one of his agents tottering, falling, with blood gushing over his collar. A second ran past, firing. Almost instantly, the third darted to the door of the valve-room, blurted to Jimmy Christopher!

"J-8 killed, sir! He was guarding the entrance to the elevator. The men have gone into it—all of them!"

"They're going up, then!" Operator 5 exclaimed.

"Yes, sir!"

"Guard this valve!"

Operator 5 jerked to the walk and glimpsed black-uniformed men rushing out of opened doors. They flung themselves against the entrance to the elevator room, found it fastened, drew back in terror. Glimpsing the guns of the Intelligence men, they began scattering. Whistling bullets, fired by Operator 5's men to force them back into the rooms, had a startling effect. First one, then the others, scrambled over the railing and plunged into the lapping, black water!

Operator 5 turned away quickly, grimly. He jerked down the receiver of the wall telephone and touched a button labeled: *Pumps.* He heard the click of the opened line and blurted: "Chief! Is that you, Chief?"

"Z-7 speaking!"

A sigh of relief issued from Operator 5's lips. "I am in control of the master valve here, Chief! The leaders of the syndicate have gone into the elevator room here!"

"We've taken the signals at the bell station!"

"Follow their directions and lift them into the ship, Chief! We'll have them if they—"

"Wait!" Z-7 shouted. "This ship is doomed! It is going down!"

"What?"

"Part of the crew was below deck. They hid themselves and we did not spot them! An officer was with them. He must have

Plumes of fire were rolling up from the dock. Men were flinging themselves into the water!

realized that the game was up—for suddenly this ship is taking water! Fire has broken out; there are holes opened in the hull! It's thermite again—charges ignited electrically, planned against just such an emergency as this! I tell you, the ship's going down!"

Operator 5 gasped. "They intend to send the ship plunging down upon this bell! If it strikes this craft as it sinks, both of them will go to the bottom! Operate the pumps at capacity and raise the pressure here as high as possible—as quickly as possible! Send that steamer away under full steam! Once it is moving, once the pressure is up, abandon ship!"

Over the tine Z-7's voice echoed as Operator 5's orders were repeated. Jimmy Christopher strode from the valve-room, slapped the door shut, clicked the bolt into its socket. He peered around the walk, saw that the black-uniformed men had vanished. Diane seized his hand and two Intelligence men hurried to his side, one of them with an arm dangling useless with a bullet wound.

"They've all plunged into the water, sir!"

"We've got to go up the same way," Operator 5 declared, "or we may be sent to the bottom with this craft. We can do nothing more here. Quick—swim up!" He faced Diane grimly. "It's got to be done, Di. Now!"

"Of course, Jimmy," the girl said quietly—but her voice was tight with terror.

Bewildered, chilled with apprehension, the two Intelligence men followed Operator 5's moves. He stripped out of his coat, kicked off his shoes. He gripped the rail, climbed over, hung poised. Diane came to his side, her face white, her eyes wide. He directed the others grimly:

"Dive deep. You'll come up under the floor. Swim underwater to clear it. Get yourselves picked up as soon as possible. Di—!"

The girl's eyes were shining into Operator 5's. Her hand clung to his. For one short moment they forgot the danger around them, the urgency of their predicament. They forgot the Intelligence men standing near them, knew only that they were together, that the plunge into the black water in an attempt to escape the bell might separate them forever. Jimmy Christopher took Diane close in his arms and felt her body trembling. His lips pressed the warmth of hers. "Now, Di," he whispered. "Now!"

The girl steeled herself for the plunge. She took a deep breath, poised. Hers was a clean dive that carried her down into the black depths. Operator 5 glimpsed her swimming rapidly underwater, and she passed from sight. At his signal, his two men raised on the rail. They drove far down into the black depths, kicking swiftly. Jimmy Christopher brought himself up, eyes narrowed.

He was alone now on this strange craft, while doom hovered overhead—alone with an Intelligence operator who had sacrificed his life to the vital mission, who now lay dead on the steel walk.

Operator 5 leaped, cleaved the water cleanly. Cold blackness surrounded him as he executed swift powerful strokes beneath the surface. The breath locked in his lungs forced him upward and he scraped the slimy bottom of the bell. Then he felt himself rising through clear water. Swiftly he kicked upward....

FLASHING PAIN filled his body as he felt himself nearing

the surface. The dread affliction of deep-sea divers—the bends—struck through his body. Growing by the moment, the torture became unendurable. Operator 5's whole body throbbed with such pain as he had never felt before. He burst up through the surface of the sea, peered with bleared eyes at a terrifying scene.

On the billows, the steamer was now aflame—sheathed with roaring fire. Plumes of blaze were rolling up from its decks. Men were flinging themselves over the rails to escape the roaring holocaust.

Boats were skirmishing through the water. Operator 5 swam swiftly. In the flare of light he glimpsed Diane's white face. The girl's eyes were pinched with the same torture that was beating through every vein of Operator 5's body. The pain became overwhelming as he guided the girl toward a boat that swerved toward them.

Peering back, he saw that the steamer was listing heavily. Its stern was sinking—and he knew that it was only a matter of moments before it would plunge for the bottom—perhaps carrying the great bell and all the United States' gold with it...!

Hands gripped Operator 5's arms. Other men were lifting Diane. Together, they sank down, pain-wracked, the whole world a nightmare of torture. Jimmy Christopher was conscious only of faraway voices in the night wind:

"She's going down!"

"Any sign of the bell coming up?"

"No—not yet!"

"She's plunging!"

"God, if she hits the bell!"

"There's no help for it now!"

Operator 5 vaguely felt himself lifted up to the deck of a larger vessel. He heard: "Get them into the compression room—quick!" Then deeper blackness flooded his mind....

OPERATOR 5 forced his eyes open. He peered around at the barrel-like chamber into which he had been brought. Beside him, face pinched with pain, lay Diane Elliot. On the opposite side were the two Intelligence men who had accompanied him down to the great bell. The chamber was airtight. The pressure within it mounted swiftly with the turning of valves. This and this alone could save them from the torture of the bends—by increasing the pressure, then lowering it very slowly. Jimmy Christopher felt a lessening of the pain throughout his body as he raised.

In the side of the cylindrical chamber was a thick, glass window. Through it, Tim Donovan was peering anxiously. The boy forced a smile, and Operator returned it weakly. From outside came muffled voices.

"The ship's down!"

"Those men in the masks—they're getting away!"

"Let 'em—they deserve the break!"

"Any sign of that bell?"

"No—not yet!"

"Plenty of pressure went down into her. Maybe the ship hit her and knocked her to the bottom! It's a chance in a million—!"

"There! What's that?"

Operator 5 saw Tim Donovan turn away, peer through the gloom, and shout: "She's up!"

Operator 5 sank back, exhausted. He saw Diane stir fitfully, and his hand closed upon her cold one....

ARMORED TRUCKS paraded undercover through the streets of Washington. Armed guards rode them. One after another, they journeyed from a United States battleship to the protected portals of the Treasury building. Each discharged a priceless cargo—gold, returned to the vaults!

Within sight of this fortified treasure trove stood the historic White House. While ingot after ingot of the precious golden metal was stored safely, the President was speaking quietly in his study, over a nationwide radio network:

"Never in our history, my friends, has this nation been as strong, both defensively and financially. We face the future without fear. We face it with confidence."

As he withdrew from the microphone that had multiplied his words millions of times, he rose with a smile. Z-7 stepped to his side. Operator 5 came forward. Beside Jimmy Christopher, ex-Operator Q-6, Diane Elliot, and Tim Donovan stood as the Chief Executive extended his hand.

"All thanks to you, Operator 5!"

"Not to me alone, Mr. President," Operator 5 replied. "We could never have succeeded without Tim and Diane."

A burst of voices in the adjoining room surprised the President. Recognizing them, he chuckled, opened the connecting door. He found the Secretary of State face to face with a stocky, florid man who was rabid with indignation. Senator Duncombe was bellowing:

"You're the head of the Intelligence! You're responsible for running that band of outlaws to earth! I demand that you destroy it, sir!"

Again chuckling, the President said: "Good evening, Duncombe. I see you're back, safe and sound!"

"A damnable outrage, sir!" the Senator roared. "I was kidnapped, held against my will. I was released only an hour ago. My first act is to come here and demand that the organization known as the Hidden Hundred be stamped out!"

The Secretary of State answered stiffly: "We've done our best on the case, Senator. In spite of the fact that it is my duty to run that organization to earth, I must admit that it has rendered valuable service to the United States. Its aid in breaking up a certain secret syndicate, hostile to the United States, was invaluable. And I may say also that it rendered this nation priceless assistance by silencing your broadcast!"

The President laughed outright, and Senator Duncombe went speechless with wrath. Operator 5 felt the smouldering eyes of Z-7 upon him, and he stood unsmiling. He saw the stern eyes of the Secretary of State turn.

"Operator 5," the Secretary said, "I assigned you special orders to capture and expose the leader of the Hidden Hundred. What report have you to make?"

"I am obliged to report, sir," Jimmy Christopher answered, "that I have failed!"

"The first failure on your record," the President mused in a low tone, "and one which I, for one, forgive!"

Yet Z-7 stood silent, smouldering black eyes on Jimmy Christopher's—and Operator 5 did not smile....

CARLETON VICTOR, photo-portraitist supreme, sat at ease in his sumptuous penthouse apartment in New York. He had entered it for the first time, after a prolonged absence, only a few moments ago. Crowe fluttered about him nervously, then hastily withdrew. Now, as Victor read the evening newspaper with keen interest, the manservant glided into the room, stood at attention and sniffed anxiously.

"Yes? What is it, Crowe?"

"I—I believe, sir, that you promised me a reprimand. For failing to keep our appointment in Studio D on the Fortieth Floor of the Universal Broadcasting Building, sir. I'm very sorry, sir. Extremely sorry, sir. Under the circumstances, sir, I feel that I must resign."

"Resign?" Victor exclaimed. "Nonsense, Crowe! Consider yourself severely reprimanded—and stay. That is, if I have your assurance that it will never happen again."

"Never, sir!" Crowe declared from the bottom of his heart. "If I can possibly prevent it, sir. If, sir, I—I am not set upon by living skeletons, sir, if I may say so, sir!"

Victor answered: "I haven't the faintest idea what you're talking about, Crowe, but—the matter is dismissed. By the way—but you never read the newspapers, do you? You very well might. There are items here, for instance, which might intrigue you. This one, for instance. Bodies picked up along the coast."

"Bodies?" Crowe echoed with a shudder. "Did you say bodies, sir?"

"Yes." Victor's tone became solemn. "One was that of a man connected with the government apparently in a secret capacity.

Others were those of foreigners—the crew of a sunken ship, it is supposed. One was a foreign espionage agent named Ruffolo. Still others are supposed to be the bodies of certain European industrial magnates. But that couldn't be possible, could it, Crowe? Most amazing of all—should you care to read about it, Crowe, which I know full well you won't—is this:

"One body was that of a man killed eighteen years ago, during the war, in a crashing plane. Major Rederick Bradshaw is the name. Yet only today his body was washed ashore in Chesapeake Bay—and he was wearing a mask of the finest gold!"